D0483994

"Evoking Roald Dahl's *The Witches*, McGowan's edgy debut novel incorporates magic, clever references to the original tale, a cast of diverse characters, and Snicket-esque narration. The witch's interspersed journal entries . . . breezily, and ominously, set the book's dark tone. Periodic shadowy illustrations add unsettling eeriness to this open-ended story that will likely draw fans of shivery, suspenseful mysteries."

—*Booklist*

"Readers know what's in store for Sol and Connie right from the riveting opening line. . . . Tanaka's occasional full-page views of grim, heavy-lidded figures add a suitably gothic tone. Yum."

—*Kirkus Reviews*

"Nuanced, fascinating, and gratifyingly dark . . . Sol and Connie are appealing in their individuality."

—*The Bulletin of the Center for Children's Books*

The
WITCH'S
CURSE

KEITH McGOWAN

with illustrations by YOKO TANAKA

Christy Ottaviano Books

HENRY HOLT AND COMPANY • NEW YORK

Henry Holt and Company, LLC
Publishers since 1866
175 Fifth Avenue
New York, New York 10010
mackids.com

Library of Congress Cataloging-in-Publication Data
McGowan, Keith.
The witch's curse / Keith McGowan ; with illustrations by Yoko Tanaka. —
First edition.
pages   cm
"Christy Ottaviano Books."
Summary: "A shadowy witch, a cursed hunter—it's tricky business for Sol
and Connie as they face off against this awful pair"—Provided by publisher.
ISBN 978-0-8050-9324-7 (hardcover)—
ISBN 978-0-8050-9750-4 (e-book)
[1. Brothers and sisters—Fiction.   2. Witches—Fiction.
3. Characters in literature—Fiction.   4. Blessing and cursing—Fiction.]
I. Tanaka, Yoko, illustrator.   II. Title.
PZ7.M478487Wh 2013
[Fic]—dc23
2012027358

First Edition—2013 / Designed by April Ward
Printed in the United States of America by R. R. Donnelley & Sons Company,
Harrisonburg, Virginia

1 3 5 7 9 10 8 6 4 2

For my mom,
Carla

The
WITCH'S
CURSE

THE HUNTER

I DON'T WISH to hunt animals who were once children. But I must. I'm woken from my long sleep by Monique, the witch of these woods, and told whom I have to hunt next. I'm cursed, you see.

It's a terrible fate.

If you are a child, you might well ask, What kind of terrible fate is that? We are the ones being turned into animals and hunted, not you. And I admit it. Those I gallop after, bow in hand, have it worse than I do.

It's worse to be hunted than to be the hunter.

Still, you can't imagine what it's like being me. When I halt by the river so my horse can drink and I see my face reflected in the rippling currents, a villain staring back. I never wanted to be a villain. I was going to settle down to a grand estate—my family's—with forty servants and a dozen carriages. Centuries ago, you see, I was a wealthy young man and, besides, a great hunter of animals. There's nothing wrong with that, is there?

My friends and I would ride into this valley. We'd blow our hunting horns, daring the animals to run from us. We always gave them a fighting chance, you see? Then we'd chase them down on our horses. It was a thrill, showing off our skills as horsemen and archers. I was the most skilled of all and proud of it.

Had I heard these woods were accursed? Yes, I'd heard that children shouldn't enter the valley. There were rumors—of lost children disappearing and an evil witch who lived here. But I never saw the witch or any evil creature. And I wasn't a child. None of us hunters were.

I thought, What does it have to do with me?

I learned soon enough, though, that the terrible fate

of the children was tied to my own fate, as tight as my horse to its bit. That some of the animals we hunted WERE the lost children, transformed into woodland beasts by the witch Monique. I should have known. It should have been obvious. But they ran from our horn blasts and our horses just like the other animals. There was nothing in their eyes to warn me when I took an arrow from my quiver, nocked it, drew back my bow-string, aimed, and let the arrow fly.

Now I am cursed because of it, and the absolute worst thing about my curse is ... knowing the truth. That the animals I now hunt—with my special arrows— once were children, they played childish games, and, just maybe, they lay alone at night, watched shadows on the wall, and dreamed of evil creatures that might soon be chasing them, like me.

So I am writing in this logbook of mine with the hope that it might someday get out of this accursed valley—I do not know how.

So that children may learn.

Because, children, I am NOT pleased to meet you.

And if by chance you ever do see my face, the one I see in the river when my horse stops to drink, then do me one big favor—if you can remember it.

Run! As fast as your legs will carry you. All four of them. I fear, though, that by then it will be too late....

⸙

SO wrote David Bittworth one summer night in his stone lodge in the mountains, far from town or city. He wrote in a small book he called his log, using a stubby pencil he sharpened himself with the sharp blade of his cooking knife. Around him stood animals, forever still: a bear, a fox, a huge caribou, an opossum, an armadillo, a duck, rabbits and weasels and beavers; near the door that opened to the mountainside stood two wolves—they had been sisters, Lisa and Nicki. So many still eyes staring at him or at the crackling flames in the fireplace or out the dark window, depending on where they were posed.

Preserved, Monique called it.

David leaned back, stretching his feet in comfortable slippers toward the fire. He wore a white nightrobe that hung from his broad shoulders. He looked very strong. He closed the logbook and kept it on the arm of his chair, the firelight flickering over it, until he rose and went to the leather bag of arrows that hung near the hearth. He took that bag down—his *quiver*—drew out the magic arrows, and stuck the small book and pencil into the bottom. He put the arrows back, checking each as he did for straightness. Only the straightest arrows were good for the hunt. They flew accurately through the air then, and struck whatever he aimed at.

Or *whoever*.

Unlucky children, he thought.

CHAPTER

SOL AND CONNIE
HIT THE ROAD

SOLOMON AND CONSTANCE BLINK—Sol and Connie
for short—hiked up a lonely country road. Sol was
eleven and Connie was eight, going on nine. Sol's
shoelace was coming untied. Connie's jumper was
twisted, and no matter how many times she'd tried to
pull it straight, it didn't feel right. Dirt smudges
covered her arms.

Knapsacks bulged on their backs. Sol slung his in
front of him to unzip it and push a water bottle back
inside. They'd already drunk more than half their
water, and the sun had dropped behind the mountains. It was getting late.

It had been Sol's idea to leave Grand Creek on
their own, set off on this road toward the looming
western mountains, to cross the bridge and enter

these woods. Sol had checked the bus schedule in town and asked. There was supposed to be one more bus leaving Grand Creek today and driving up this road. That bus would head west through the mountains to the city where Sol and Connie's aunt Heather lived. Sol thought they could trust their aunt Heather—their mother's sister—much more than they could trust their father and stepmother, Mr. and Mrs. Blink, whom they were leaving behind.

They would flag the bus down when it passed.

That had been Sol's idea.

"It should come soon," he said to Connie, glancing back down the road for the thousandth time as they walked. It had been more than two hours since they'd started hiking.

Connie nodded. She trusted her older brother maybe more than he trusted himself.

Sol, on the other hand, didn't totally trust Connie. He cared for her, of course, loved her, and could name many of her good qualities. He would always watch out for her. But it was just a fact, as Sol saw it: Sometimes his younger sister could be tricky.

"Aunt Heather will be surprised to see us," said Connie.

"Very surprised," Sol said.

"When was the last time we saw her?" she asked.

"Five years ago."

"I hardly remember her."

"She's nice," Sol said. "I hope."

Connie hesitated, then finally asked, "And Dad?"

Sol didn't know what to say. He just shook his head and crouched to tie his shoelace.

Connie didn't ask again. They'd have time to talk about it all later, or so she thought.

Sol pulled the knot tight on his sneaker. He stood and looked back along the empty road for the thousand-and-first time.

No bus.

They hiked on, believing that the more distance they put between themselves and Grand Creek, the better.

EARLIER THAT DAY

AS TO THEIR FATHER, Mr. Blink, Sol *had* tried to write a goodbye note to him before they'd fled their home. Sol and Connie had been packing hurriedly in their shared bedroom. There had been little time to spare. Still, Sol had wasted a moment to find a paper and pencil and write the note.

As he did, he glanced out the bedroom window at the house next door: Fay Holaderry's house, twisty vines climbing up its side. Holaderry was the reason Sol and Connie were leaving. She was an evil witch who cooked and ate children—sometimes with fine cloth napkins and candles lit, other times sitting in the glow of prime-time TV and snacking from the plate on her lap. She had caught Connie that very day, then Sol, tied them up in her secret underground kitchen, and gotten so far as to heat the sauce she would eat them with—a marjoram goulash—before Sol and Connie had gotten out of her house.

They'd pushed her into her fire pit. They should have been safe. But every time Sol or Connie glanced through the window at her house, it was hard for them not to imagine her face appearing suddenly in one of the windows. Just the thought of it was frightening. Also, Holaderry had magical helpers in Grand Creek who looked like ordinary people. So Sol and Connie had decided to pack and leave as soon as possible, as in *right now that very second*.

Even so, Sol took a moment to sit on the lower bunk bed and write his father the note. Neither their father nor their stepmother was at home. Connie stood beside him and read over his shoulder.

This is what Sol wrote:

Dear Dad,
We are leaving right away. Grand Creek isn't safe.
Get out as quickly as you can. We'll meet later, and I
can explain it all to you then.
Your son, Sol
PS—Don't worry about the babysitter, she's been
taken care of.

Even before he finished the note, though, Sol realized he hardly meant a word of it. One clue to that was that he did not mention where they were going—to Aunt Heather's. It was as if he didn't want his dad to know. Actually, Sol thought, he didn't. He understood then what he'd kept pushed into the tiniest corner of his mind at least since the night he'd overheard a private conversation between his father and stepmother.

Sol and Connie's parents had been cooperating with Holaderry.

Sol saw that he hadn't even written *Love, Sol*, at the

end of his note, just *Your son, Sol.* Did he even love his father, he wondered? Actually, Sol should have been wondering about the *Your son* part too. But he never suspected even then that the man he called his father was really his uncle.

Sol wondered what he should do about the note. He wasn't sure, so he put it aside for the moment on the little table by the bed.

"Ten minutes, one bag," he said, turning to Connie.

But instead of going back to packing, Connie chose exactly then to head out of the bedroom.

"Where are you going?" Sol asked.

"If we're catching a bus, we'll need snacks," she said, stopping in the doorway.

"Okay, good thinking. Bring a bottle of water too," Sol said. "But hurry—we've got to get out of here."

"I *am* hurrying. You're the one wasting time, asking me questions." And with that, Connie rushed down the hall.

Trying to forget the note, Sol went to his knapsack. Cardboard boxes were stacked everywhere in the room. Sol and Connie's family had arrived in

Grand Creek only two days before, and they'd hardly had time to unpack their boxes from the move. Sol was faced with the question: What was it that was most important to him? Even before writing his note, Sol had already packed the most important thing of all: old yellowing papers—his mother's last scientific publication. Sol and Connie's mother had been a brilliant scientist, one of the earliest to predict global warming and the melting of the ice shelf in Antarctica. But she'd fallen into the Antarctic Ocean while conducting her research and was never heard from again.

There'd been a time when Sol had imagined that his mother wasn't really gone—that she would come walking through the door one day. But Sol was, above all, logical, and he had finally admitted to himself on his eleventh birthday that such a wish was not. What he had left from her were some photos and videos, stored online, and this original copy of her final treatise.

No, Sol thought now, he had something else from his mother too. What he'd inherited from her: scientific smarts.

Glancing at cardboard boxes full of his scientific

belongings, Sol knew that he couldn't take any of them with him. He had already thrown clothes into his knapsack on top of his mom's scientific paper, plus Holaderry's leather-bound journal, which they had stolen from the witch's house during a break-in. That journal had information in it and stories from Holaderry's life. He could never have left it behind. On the very first page Holaderry had written her awful title for the journal: *How to Cook and Eat Children.*

He'd also packed a paperback book called *The Mismeasure of Man,* and then he added a little blank notebook that he thought might come in handy—the notebook he'd torn paper out of to write the note for his father.

He tossed in the pencil too.

There simply wasn't much room left in his knapsack. He couldn't possibly pack his telescope, his microscope, or his most complex invention to date—his heat detection device, which was still outside on Holaderry's lawn anyway. And he had no time to waste looking through all of his boxes.

Still Sol dug through one box and found, just where he thought it was, a small black cube. He smiled—something he hadn't done the whole time he was packing. That cube was a computer he'd built long ago, with a microphone and a speaker built into it but no screen. It was one of his earliest inventions. He'd named it his Know-It-All Cube. This, then, was what he wanted to take with him—for sentimental reasons, really, he realized. He hadn't used it in over a year.

"On," he said to it.

"Cube on," it said back in his own voice. He had recorded all of the words it spoke himself.

He was surprised that its batteries still had some charge in them. Good batteries, he told himself, were very important.

"Off," he said to it.

"Off," it said in his voice. He'd forgotten to put a light on it when he'd built it, so Sol had to trust that the cube had turned itself off. Still, if it hadn't, Sol knew, it would speak up after a while.

He stuffed it into his knapsack, then thought of something else he wanted to bring with him—something else that couldn't be replaced. A Valentine's Day card he'd gotten in his class last year from a secret valentine. It was the only card like that he'd ever gotten in his life. Sol wasn't the kind of boy who normally got valentine cards from girls. That card was scientific proof that at least one girl *had* liked him at his old school after all.

Where had he hidden it? Inside one of his books. He had to flick through the pages of three—time was ticking—until he found it inside a thick tome on meteorology.

Connie came back just as Sol was putting the valentine card into his pack. He put it in quickly. He'd never shown it to his little sister. That would just have been embarrassing.

Connie gave him a water bottle and a small bag of potato chips—she'd brought two. Sol packed his bag of chips and the bottle.

"Come on, hurry up," he said to Connie.

<hr />

CONNIE, feeling the pressure, went quickly to her knapsack. She had a simple plan for packing fast. She wasn't going to bring that much.

Anyway, she'd already packed the three things most important to her.

Those were: (1) a figurine of the Monster from the Deep, with fake seaweed dripping off of it, that she liked to stand on her dresser; (2) a framed photo of her old cat, Quantum, whom she'd had to give away to a friend before they'd moved to Grand Creek; and (3) her favorite pair of socks, which she called her *snake socks* because they had a diamond pattern on them that she thought looked like snake scales.

Connie packed her bag of potato chips and a few more clothes, including a warm sweater, although it was the last day of August. Then she stepped between boxes to where something very important lay, leaning against the bunk bed.

An ancient cane.

THEY had grabbed the cane just after running out of Holaderry's secret underground kitchen. In a short hallway outside the kitchen had stood a glass cabinet full of strange objects, including a giant ceramic flower; a tiger statue leaning against an old-style mirror; a denim vest painted with the words *Rattlers #61*, a rattlesnake, and a skull; and the ancient wood cane, its handle carved in the shape of a duck's head.

Before they had rushed up the stairs to escape, Sol had said, "Doesn't that cane remind you of someone?"

"Definitely," Connie had answered.

So they'd opened the glass doors quickly, taken the cane, then run up the stairs and carried it back with them.

Now Connie picked it up and wondered, What if they had taken some of the other things in the cabinet too? But they'd been in a rush to get out of Holaderry's house. The cane *had* been most important. Its duck's head did remind her of someone—a woman they had met in Grand Creek who ran a shop called All Creatures, Big and Small, and who walked with a normal, modern cane. Connie thought of that woman as *the only nice person in all of Grand Creek*. They were going to bring this ancient cane to her.

The cane wouldn't fit in Connie's knapsack, though. So, she thought, I'm done packing. Except, she realized, there was one other thing she was bringing with her that also didn't go in her knapsack, or anywhere at all. It was this: a secret she should probably tell Sol soon, she thought, after seeing what he had packed. She hoped Sol wouldn't be too upset.

Connie hefted her knapsack onto her shoulders. Hers was green. Sol's was red. Sol did the same. He glanced at the note on the side table, picked it up, crumpled it into a ball, and stuffed it into his back pocket. The second he did, Sol and Connie were officially on the run. And so they fled their new home.

Sol took the cane from Connie's hand while they walked through town to the shop All Creatures, Big and Small. When they arrived, it was closed. Outside was a tree full of chattering birds. Sol and Connie banged on the glass of the shop but no one answered. A flyer in the window read ANSWER 3 RIDDLES AND WIN A PRIZE, and written by hand below was GOOD LUCK, YOU TWO.

Sol and Connie hoped that was meant for them. Sol tore a page out of his notebook, wrote THANK YOU, and signed it. Connie signed it too, adding her own THANKS! They stuck the note on the duck's bill, left the cane leaning against the shop door, and went on.

So it is that when you flee somewhere, you escape not only whatever bad it is you're running from, but also the good people you've come to know. As they walked away, Sol wondered, Would there be anyone to help them on the road ahead?

They checked in the center of town for bus times, but the last bus wasn't leaving yet. So they'd struck out on the road, wanting to get out of town fast. They could flag the bus down when it passed, Sol told

Connie. They came to a bridge with rushing water beneath it. A wooden sign told them that was Grand Creek itself, the creek that the town was named for.

After the bridge, the road narrowed and the woods grew wilder. A NO TRESPASSING sign, nailed high on a tree to one side, had the NO part crossed out with black paint. So it read simply TRESPASSING.

"Just some vandals," Sol had said to Connie.

Huge rocks lay among the trees, the kind one might normally sit on to rest. But Sol and Connie hadn't rested. Two hours later, they were still hiking up the road. Mountains loomed ahead. The sun had fallen behind the highest peak to the west. Sol and Connie looked back often and hoped the bus would come soon.

⁂

PAST those western peaks, a shadow was creeping along the mountainside—that was Monique, the witch of the woods, the queen of the accursed valley. She could always sense when more children were coming her and David's way. As she moved into a clearing of broken rocks high over the valley, nothing of her could be seen. She was just a shadow that slid over the land—as if a patch of night was walking through the day. Because Monique could be seen only when she wanted to be seen. It was said the mere sight of her turned one to stone.

But that was just rumor. For Monique to freeze you, she had to recite a spell or enchant an arrow. A person could look on her and live. She wasn't always a shadow.

In the trees around that high rocky clearing, hundreds of crows weighed down the branches. You might think that those crows were in league with Monique, but that wasn't true. The crows just liked to watch whenever something was happening in the accursed valley or on the mountain slopes.

The shadow drifted over to a narrow mountain spring burbling between boulders. Herbs, seeds, powders, fur, and other strange things fell out of the shadow's darkness, landing atop the spring. Some of those items disappeared instantly when they struck the water. Others floated and were drawn spinning downstream across the clearing and into trees, feeding a wooded pool. From the pool, streams spread in many directions down the mountainside.

Little cloth bags came flying out of the shadow, as if tossed, until ten or twelve piled up to the side—all of them empty.

Apparently Monique was dumping quite a few bags of strange ingredients into the spring.

The witch's high voice came from the shadow, singing notes that ran up and down scales almost like an aria from an opera. The crows in the trees cawed when they heard her.

Monique sang,

> *Tu bois,*
> *Ma proie,*
> *Et voilà,*
> *La chasse commence.*

One didn't need to understand the French words to know that they cast a spell, or that the power of the witch's spell came not just from the words themselves but from the ingredients that had been emptied into the spring.

After the sound of the last word faded, the crows stopped cawing too. The shadow drifted over the pile of empty little bags. When it moved on, the bags were gone. Monique must have picked them up.

She drifted across the clearing and melted into the woods.

The crows flew off in a gigantic dark flock shortly after, their wings beating the air loudly. A single crow remained, though, and it flew down into the clearing. It had seen, earlier, one small bag fall and roll away from the shadow when the shadow was on its way to the spring to cast the spell. That bag stuck out now beneath the wide pointy leaves of a plant growing in the stones. The crow went to investigate, walking fast, with its head stretched in front. It pecked at the bag, which was full—the bag had never been emptied into the flowing spring. It had been accidentally dropped. The crow wedged its beak into the top and started pulling out bark, black fur, and hard seeds. Clutching the bag with the claws of one foot, it flew up to a limb. It held the bag up to its beak and pulled out seeds—the best part—and whatever came with them, until the bag slipped from its clutch.

The crow didn't try to recover the bag. Instead, it cawed to no one, as all the other crows had left. Then it shook out its feathers, puffed itself up in the breeze, turned its head around, and buried its head in its wings.

The little bag hung caught on a branch.

CHAPTER

4

A WITCH'S HELPER
ON THE BUS?

BEFORE THEY SAW anything, Sol and Connie heard
the rumble of an engine behind them. They looked
back, and a bus came around a curve, pulling out
into the middle of the road because of the sharpness
of the turn. Sol and Connie waved their hands over
their heads, more like stranded travelers trying to be
seen by a search plane than like two kids signaling for
a bus, driving right by them, to stop.

"It'll stop," Sol said to Connie, waving his arms
very high.

The bus screeched to a halt. Its brakes squeaked
terribly loud. The whole vehicle tilted to the side as it
idled, waiting for Sol and Connie. Its bottom edge
was rusty. It looked as if that bus had seen more than
its share of snowy winters and rainy summers driving over the mountains.

The door slid open with a quiet thump when Sol and Connie reached it. The bus driver, whom they saw at the top of the steps, was a narrow woman with straight hair that brought out her thinness. Her long arms reached around the steering wheel, elbows sticking out. Her face was sharp too, but the expression on it was soft.

"Going to?" she asked them as they stepped up.

Connie looked at Sol.

Sol said, "Last stop, Newburgh."

"Okay, buy your tickets at the next town, over the mountains," she told them.

They found their seats. The bus was surprisingly full for one coming from such a small town. Though perhaps it had only passed through Grand Creek from somewhere farther east. The people looked normal enough: bags on their laps, cell phones being checked. One had a computer open, and another was putting his hand to his lips with some snack food in it.

Nothing strange at all.

But, Sol thought, any of them could be one of Holaderry's magical helpers. To the average eye, Sol knew, the helpers looked like ordinary people, even though according to Holaderry's journal, they were actually only a couple of feet tall. The witch's helpers might have heard what Sol and Connie had done to Holaderry. One or more of them *could* have gotten onto the bus in Grand Creek, Sol thought.

An older man on the bus made a kind gesture, though. He switched his seat to one across the aisle so that Sol and Connie could sit next to each other. He smiled politely but hardly looked at them, settling into his new seat and turning away.

"I want the window," Connie said.

Sol had gone in first. But he stopped and let her squeeze past. She pushed into him and accidentally jabbed him with her elbow.

"Watch out," Sol said quietly.

"Sorry," Connie said.

Sol sat and leaned back. His head bumped against the curved bottom of the headrest. The seats were made for average adult height, which he wasn't.

Connie leaned forward next to him, staring out the window. The bus started again. Its engine was very loud. They quickly gained speed. Trees flew by outside. The road curved and twisted.

Half an hour later, the bus was struggling uphill and emerged briefly out of the woods. Sol sat up straight to see out over Connie's head. They had a view of where they'd come from. Grand Creek lay in the distance, the roofs of its houses a patchwork of colors.

Both of them felt a great relief seeing that town already far off. Although, deep down, they knew that being on their way to safety and arriving there were two different things. But this was a start.

Sol leaned back and did his best to relax. Still, he couldn't help wondering again: What if one or more of the witch's helpers were following them now?

Even the old man who'd changed his seat so that Sol and Connie could sit together could have been one of them. Sol looked over, trying not to be obvious about it. He noticed that the old man's mouth closed in that funny way mouths close when they have no teeth, shortening the whole head. But this harmless-looking old man *could* be a helper in disguise, Sol knew, waiting for just the right moment to grab the two of them. Back in Grand Creek, one of Holaderry's helpers—also innocent looking—had captured Connie when Sol had left her alone for just a few minutes.

Sol glanced over at Connie now. She was staring out the window and didn't look too nervous. He tried to relax.

Actually, at that moment, Connie *was* worrying as she gazed at Grand Creek in the distance. But she was worrying about other things besides the witch's helpers—for instance, what their aunt would be like. Connie could hardly recall Aunt Heather. It had been so long since they'd last seen her.

Connie was also worrying about the secret she had to tell Sol after seeing him pack that Valentine's Day card. Sol wouldn't be happy to hear the truth, Connie was sure. That made her lips turn down just to think about it.

Connie was worrying too about something much more immediate: the curvy mountain road that the bus was on now, which, it seemed to her, wasn't safe at all. Outside her window, the road's edge dropped off like a cliff. The bus was driving close to the edge, sometimes *very* close as the driver steered without paying attention, it seemed to Connie. They might accidentally slide off the mountain road. Then, just like in a movie, the bus would fall, turning over and over and crashing at the bottom of the cliff, exploding into flames.

Connie could see it all in her mind.

She was brought out of those thoughts when the

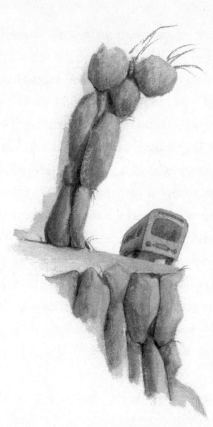

bus wheels started kicking up loose stones from the road that clattered loudly against the floor under her feet.

The bus reached a final tight curve. It struggled up a steep slope. Its engine choked under the strain and then stalled completely. For a moment, there was silence, until the engine caught again, roared, and the bus continued its climb.

At last the road leveled off. Connie saw they were driving around the mountain peak itself, which looked like a rock hill outside the window. The top of the peak was half hidden by fog that was actually, Connie thought, a cloud. That's how high they were.

They drove around a very long curve. Then they were beyond the peak. And whatever Connie or Sol expected, they didn't expect what they saw. Instead of being past the mountains and seeing towns and cities ahead, they were at the start of a mountain range. Ahead, more peaks loomed in the distance. Before them stretched a wooded valley every shade of green from the lightest to the darkest, with a winding river at its center.

The road dropped at once. Sol and Connie saw nothing but trees again flashing by on both sides. The bus shuddered as it gained speed.

INTO THE WOODS

A LITTLE LATER, Connie was nodding off and Sol was looking past her at the trees flying by when a burst sounded from under the bus. The bus wobbled violently.

The driver braked.

"Flat tire," she announced.

The groans of the people and the way they stood up, mumbling to each other, suggested that they weren't surprised.

"At least it's only a flat," one man near Sol and Connie said. "Did you hear the engine?"

Others nodded and mumbled in agreement.

"Everyone off," the driver said.

They filed off the bus. They were in the mountain valley. The air was fresh. A wind blew across the road. Leaves rustled in the trees by the roadside. Behind them, they could see the mountain they had driven over, its peak close.

Sol fell in with a group of people gathering around the flat tire to watch the driver change it.

"Sol," Connie said from beside him, "I've got to pee."

Sol nodded without turning to her. He was watching the driver walk over with a large rock she'd found. She stuck it behind one of the front wheels. That would keep the bus from rolling once it was raised on the jack, Sol knew.

"Come with me, Sol," Connie said.

Now he turned to look at her.

"Not all the way," she said. "Just nearby."

Sol answered with disappointment in his voice. "Okay."

The driver was pulling the jack from a side compartment on the bus. It was a hydraulic jack, Sol saw. That meant it would use liquid pressure to lift the bus. He was always interested in these things—how a thin woman could lift a whole bus with help from science. The driver slammed the compartment shut with a high squeak that echoed across the road.

Sol tried to keep watching as he and Connie walked to the road's uneven edge, but the group of people by the wheel closed around the driver.

On the roadside, other passengers stood, stepping restlessly or checking their cell phones. Judging by the way they frowned at the phones and held them up, as if the phones were instruments for measuring the clouds in the sky, they couldn't get a signal.

Sol noticed the old man without teeth too, near the front of the bus, looking around. When the man glanced in Sol and Connie's direction, he started walking casually their way. Connie was already squeezing between leafy bushes, her jumper pulled from side to side as she did. Sol followed, pushing branches out of his face, the forest floor crunching under his sneakers, a sound that could just be heard under the rustling of leaves in the wind. They were going downhill. His long hair got tangled in branches, and he had to reach behind him several times to tug it free.

He called out, "Here's good, Connie."

Connie looked back.

"But I can still see people," she said.

Sol peered through the trees behind them. He

could see a few heads and bodies through the branches.

"So?" he asked.

"So, Sol, you're the scientific genius," Connie said. "If I can see them, *they* can see *me*."

Sol shook his head, but he held his tongue. He saw that the old man was by the edge of the woods, staring in as if looking for them. The man even stepped a little into the woods himself. Although he didn't seem to be able to find them. Here it must be said that this old man, not wearing his teeth that day, was simply looking out for Sol and Connie. And, if you are on the run from witches or other evil creatures, it may cause you almost as much harm to suspect a person who means you well as to trust someone who doesn't. But how can you tell the difference between the two?

"Okay," Sol decided, "keep going, but just a little more." He added, "And stay quiet."

They walked on. When the wind gusted, the tree branches shook around them. Suddenly an elk was in front of them—or rather, they surprised it as they stepped around some bushes. It was almost as big as a bull. Long, bony branching antlers grew from its head. Its muscles were thick and powerful. In its eyes,

Sol saw surprise and something else. . . . Anger? Fear? Warning?

It turned and ran into the woods, not as quickly as a smaller animal might have, but fast enough and strong in each step. Connie and Sol took a few steps after it so that they could see it as it ran away. They watched until it was gone from sight and all they saw was brush shaking in the distance. They heard far-away crashing.

"Did you see how big those horns were?" Connie said, holding her hands wide over her head to show just how big.

"They're antlers, not horns," Sol corrected her.

He didn't mention a feeling he had about these woods and especially the way the animal had looked at him. He glanced up at the straight clouds skittering overhead, low over the treetops. He listened and heard a bird singing three notes and another making a clicking sound. He looked around, and nothing seemed strange. But he didn't see the road or people anymore. They had moved too far when they saw the elk.

"You should go now, Connie," he said.

"Okay," she said.

She pushed through close-together bushes and stepped behind a wide tree. Sol could hear her moving around back there. He didn't like to lose sight of her, but what should he do?

Besides, he had to go himself.

⁂

WHEN he finished his business, zipping up, he noticed a crow watching him from a branch. It stretched its head out and cawed at him. Then it opened its wings, which made it look very big, jumped up to another branch, and took off.

"Connie? Connie?"

"Hang on, Sol," she called. She appeared, coming through the bushes head down, arms in front, pushing her way through.

"Come on, let's get out of here," Sol said at once.

But he started in one direction, and Connie another.

"It's *that* way," they both said at the same time, pointing in different directions.

Sol thought about it.

"You could be off a little to the right, and I might be off to the left," he said. "What we should do logically, then, is take the average of our mistakes."

He judged where Connie was pointing and where he was pointing, and picked the direction exactly in the middle of the two.

"Let's go," he said.

It was difficult to walk just that way. Sol and Connie were blocked by logs lying on their sides with dead, crooked branches sticking up. Sol had to keep turning. They both got scratched, and their knapsacks sometimes got stuck. They had to free themselves with a tug. When Sol and Connie finally got through and could go straight, they may or may not have been headed in the same direction as before. Though Sol judged that they were—or close.

A steep hill of pine trees rose ahead of them. Sol bent his legs a lot as he climbed, and pushed himself up straight with each step. For Connie it was even more effort, although she had the advantage of being smaller and lighter.

When they reached the top, though, there was no road. Only a pond, dark gray, reflecting the clouds.

Crows began to fly in and were landing on the trees, from the lowest branches to the highest ones. Rows and rows of crows. To Sol they looked almost like they were an audience—some with the high seats and some with the low seats—out to see a show. An audience that cawed to each other.

Sol glanced over at Connie and then he suddenly smiled.

"I'm so stupid," he said. "I forgot, I brought my Know-It-All Cube with me. It's been so long since I made it. It has a function for this."

He took his knapsack off, unzipped it, and pulled out the small black cube. Since he wasn't looking at Connie, he didn't notice her worried expression.

"I'm going to get us out of here," Sol said.

THE KNOW-IT-ALL CUBE

HE BROUGHT THE CUBE to his mouth.

"On," he spoke into it.

"Cube on," it said back in his own voice.

"Menu," Sol said.

"Menu selected," it answered. "Encyclopedia mode, puzzle mode, math mode, melody mode—"

Sol interrupted it.

"GPS mode," he said.

"Connie mode selected."

Sol's eyebrows scrunched down. He looked at Connie.

"Stop," Sol said to the cube.

"Stopped," it said back in his voice.

"*I* never made a Connie mode," he said to Connie.

Connie made a face, a tight smile with her eyes

widened. Sol understood that she meant: I'm embar-
rassed, but it's not so important, is it? Isn't it sort of
funny?

What Connie said was this: "It was ages ago, Sol.
I heard you talking to it. It was funny the way you say
anything to it, and it talks back and sounds exactly
like you—"

Sol held up his hand to her and said, "Stop,"
sounding a lot like when he talked to the cube. He
brought the cube up to his lips again.

"Menu," he said.

"Menu selected," the cube said back in Sol's voice.
"Encyclopedia mode—"

"GPS mode," Sol said.

"Connie mode selected," it said back.

Sol paused.

"Connie mode run," he said.

"Connie mode run," it said in his voice. "Connie
is great. Connie is fun. Connie is smart. Connie is
nice—"

"Stop," Sol said.

"Stopped," it said back.

He lowered it to his waist. He stuck his hand into
his hair by his scalp, not to run his hand through his
hair but just to hold it there and pull.

"How many times have I told you not to touch my stuff?"

"A lot?" Connie guessed.

"A lot? A million times. A quadrillion times. A septillion times. A—" He stopped. "And now—*now* you see why?" His voice was reaching a strangled tone. It was rare that Sol got that upset.

Connie nodded, not looking into his eyes.

"What did you *do* to it?" Sol asked.

"I programmed it, just like you do," Connie said. She sounded a tiny bit proud of herself, although she didn't want to. "I heard how you did it—through the door," she admitted. "I can do things like that too. I'm good at remembering what I hear."

"Connie, I want you to listen to this thing." Sol suddenly became teacherly. He brought the cube closer. "Connie mode run," he told it.

"Connie mode run," the cube said back in his voice. "Connie is great. Connie is fun. Connie is smart. Connie is nice. Connie is the best sister in the world. I love Connie. Connie is funny. I will serve Connie. I am Connie's servant. With my help, Connie will rule the world—"

"Stop," Sol said.

"Stopped," the cube said.

"Do you hear this?" Sol asked Connie.

Connie nodded.

"Do you think this is doing what I do? What I do is make useful programs, programs that help people, programs that *do* something. What does your program do?"

"I thought it was fun, Sol, that's all," Connie said. "To hear your voice saying all those things."

"For that, you ruined my cube? So you could hear me say I'm your servant?"

"Well, you never say that normally."

Sol spread his hands to either side, as if he were going to grab Connie's head or slam her on her ears.

"What did you do to it, anyway? Why can't I get into the rest of it?"

"I don't know. I think it blew out or something. I may have dropped it," she said very quietly.

"Dropping it shouldn't have hurt it. It's shockproof, waterproof, magnetproof, heatproof—"

"I don't know, Sol. I guess I did something to it."

Sol stared at the ground, then up. He breathed out loudly.

"GPS mode," he said one more time to the cube.

"Connie mode selected."

"Stop."

"Stopped," it said.

"Off," Sol said.

"Off," it said back.

"I hope you're happy."

Sol put it back into the knapsack, which he slung

onto his shoulders. He had a serious, troubled look in his eyes.

"We have to do this carefully, Connie." He put his hand to his lips, pulling it away a little later. "Every step we take in the wrong direction, it's a step that could take us farther away from the road, instead of closer. If we've been going the wrong way this whole time, we could be twice as far from the road as we were. And we don't have any way to judge. I don't have a compass. There are other ways to judge directions, by the sun, the stars, or moss that grows more on the north side of trees if it's shady. But I'm not sure of the direction we came from, so none of that matters. And there is no sun, it's past the mountains already, although I'd say it's over there somewhere. That area must be westerly, but it could be northwesterly or southwesterly, it's hard to tell. And there are no stars. No moss."

It was only then that a thought occurred to Connie.

"But, Sol," Connie asked, "won't the bus wait for us?"

"I don't know," Sol said, frustrated. "It's not a school bus. We're on our own now, Connie. We have to take care of ourselves." He looked at her. "*I* have to take care of *you*. They might think we got on the bus just to ride it down the road." He snorted. "We didn't even pay!"

Sol looked so upset that Connie felt truly bad.

"Sol," she said, "I think I know the logical thing to do now."

Sol looked at her.

"Shout," she said. "We should shout."

CHAPTER

GERTRUDE RETURNS

SOL CONSIDERED IT. "You're right, Connie. It's a good idea," he admitted. "If we're close enough, they'll hear us."

So Sol and Connie started shouting as loud as they could, things like "We're here!" and "Don't go-o-o!"

Connie's shouts, in particular, were howls, as if she were being dragged away by wolves that very second. Sol thought to tell her to calm down, but he knew what she'd say. They wanted to be heard, didn't they? So he tried to scream just as loud as Connie, to sound just as desperate. But doing that only brought a bad feeling on.

MEANWHILE, in Grand Creek, a centuries-old woman was stepping up to the back door of her shop with four dogs, and she had Sol and Connie on her mind. She looked almost as big as a bear, and she walked with a cane. Her name was Gertrude Bredbord.

The last time she'd seen Sol and Connie was in the afternoon. She'd known that Fay Holaderry was close to capturing and cooking the children, but Gertrude hadn't been able to help. That was the hardest part of her life, seeing kids in need in Grand Creek and standing aside.

She'd been unable to help kids escape Holaderry ever since she'd lost her homemade cane to that witch more than a century ago. She had lost the cane during a struggle in a thunderstorm—two women in a knock-down brawl, and Gertrude had come up the loser. Fay Holaderry had been able to curse Gertrude after that, since the cane was an object of great importance to Gertrude. From then on, all Gertrude could do was drop little hints for the children or tell them riddles. Riddles were always allowed—as long as they were difficult to solve, of course—according to the ancient rules she and Holaderry lived by.

Gertrude was also allowed to make small gestures. Holaderry couldn't stop her from doing that. For instance, she'd given Sol and Connie a dog treat yesterday. She didn't know if it had been of any help. It wasn't much compared to what she should have been able to do.

After seeing the children again this afternoon, Gertrude had decided to send a bird—a little wood thrush—to see what happened to them and to report back.

But the thrush hadn't returned, and Gertrude feared the worst: that Sol and Connie were being cooked right that minute for Holaderry's supper.

She was thinking that as she opened her shop's back door. The four dogs ran in at once, across the back landing, up two steps, through a small animal training room, and into the shop itself, where their water bowls were tucked into a corner. She followed them in, her plain cane clicking as she walked. She was lost in thought—thinking how it was her fate to make do with so little. She was an unlucky woman.

Pech, she thought in German, one of the many languages she knew. It meant, roughly speaking, "tough luck."

Gertrude walked through the aisles of animal products that she sold—cat collars, chew bones, birdhouses, fish tanks—and sank into her chair by the till, or *cash register*, as it was called nowadays. She told herself that Sol and Connie might not end up like the others. There were a few lucky kids who got away.

The four dogs lapped up their water and then sprawled out on the floor. Their ears perked up as the front windows rattled—a wind was rising—though they didn't move from their comfortable positions. The rattling windows reminded Gertrude how she had tried to comfort herself that day by writing a note for Sol and Connie on a paper in the front window, before leaving on her walk. She'd imagined that they might read it.

But the thrush hadn't come back.

Well, she thought, wood thrushes were unreliable birds. Their memories were short. The thrush might have been distracted along the way.

Gertrude heard a clattering outside then, near the door, which was odd, because there was nothing out there to fall over. It must be a branch from the tree, fallen in the wind, she thought. She would clear it up later.

Then she heard the rattling of the front panes again. No, not a rattling this time, a *tap-tap-tap, tap-tap-tap.*

The thrush!

She rose from her chair and went to the front door to pull it open. The thrush flew in over Gertrude's shoulder. But Gertrude's eye was caught by something else—what lay on the sidewalk before her shop. She took a couple of steps to stand over it: an ancient cane with a piece of paper stuck on its bill. Gertrude stood dumbfounded in the wind for at least a minute. It was her cane. She hadn't seen it in so many years—over a hundred. The sight of the cane brought a surge of hope to her. There was no doubt about it. Even without reading the note, she knew who'd brought the cane back to her. It had been in Holaderry's house, and obviously Sol and Connie had gone into the house and made it out again.

Still, Gertrude's feelings on seeing the cane weren't totally good. Because her cane was missing something. Two things, actually. Its eyes. Gertrude had carved the cane herself, painstakingly, hundreds of years ago, and when she'd finished it, she had glued in two black buttons for eyes—buttons she'd had ever since she was a girl. It was the button eyes that gave the cane much of its power, coming from her childhood as they did.

And Holaderry had been clever—Holaderry was always clever. She'd known where the power lay too. She must have pried those button eyes off right away when she'd brought the stolen cane back home, and hidden them somewhere else.

Without its eyes, the cane wasn't fully returned to Gertrude. Still, she hoped to feel some of her strength come back to her when she bent and picked it up. But all she felt, *leider*, was the pain in her leg—why she walked with the cane in the first place—and a secondary pain shooting up in her back. Her sciatic nerve. Drat! She straightened up, her face darkened with pain. She pulled the note off the bill and read it. That, at least, made her smile, if a bit crookedly.

"No," she said. "Thank *you*."

She stepped back into her shop, closing the door and sitting down again in her chair. She leaned her more modern cane against the wall. She wouldn't need it anymore.

Her mind turned to new thoughts.

Sol and Connie had escaped, but where had they gone?

Her eyes found the thrush, which had landed on the till—exactly on the button that opened the money drawer with a *ding*. Startled by the sound, the thrush had flown down to the slippery countertop.

The little brown and white bird looked at Gertrude.

"Tell me," Gertrude said to it.

The thrush chattered and sang, and Gertrude listened. Its sounds formed images in her mind. The thrush's story was a bit confused in the telling, with many odd details that were of importance only to a small bird. What Gertrude understood was, first, that the thrush had seen the children run from Holaderry's house to their own little apartment building next door. Next, that Holaderry had appeared sometime later in her bedroom window upstairs with a badly blistered face.

"That won't matter," Gertrude told the thrush. "Once kids escape a witch, she won't chase after them. Fair is fair. Besides, there are always more children where those two came from."

The thrush kept singing and calling. Sol and Connie had set off along the western road, and the bird had followed them until they had boarded a bus. That's what had taken it so long.

"It's okay if you stopped for a snack," Gertrude

told it. "You did well. That was a big undertaking for you."

Her expression grew serious. Her bottom lip turned in. Her forehead rose.

"So, we're in the middle, not the end," she said. "Sol and Connie are headed straight for Monique and her hunter on that old bus. She'll never let them through." Gertrude blew out through her thick lips. "I knew there was a reason you wrote to me, Lenore," she said, a faraway look in her eyes.

She stood, but before she went to search for the letter Lenore had sent her long ago, Gertrude stepped over to where packets of birdseed lay on her shelves. Abruptly she smiled, because it was something wonderful to walk leaning on her ancient cane, feeling the smooth bumps of the duck's head—eyes or no eyes, power or no power. She took one packet of birdseed, then a second. She opened them and, coming back, poured their contents onto the countertop. The thrush immediately went to work pecking at the seeds, sending many of them flying off the counter to the floor.

As Gertrude watched it, an idea formed in her mind. Her cane wasn't in one piece, and the most important part had been left behind. But she still had most of it back, and that should mean some of her power was returned—some of the curse broken. Or did it? Was it possible to half break a curse?

She didn't know. She would have to try to find out. She knew where to look.

Meanwhile, though, she could try something. She had to act as fast as possible—events were moving quickly. Maybe she could reach animals ahead that would help Sol and Connie in the western valley. She'd try. She held her cane tightly, closed her eyes, and concentrated. It had been a long time since she'd tried something so powerful. As soon as she did, though, she felt shadows forming in every corner of her shop. She opened her eyes and saw them circling her. If she continued, they would take form, close in, and hold her captive for days or weeks. She'd be helpless.

Gertrude breathed out and stopped. She wouldn't be able to do more. *Pech*, she thought. Why was her life always like this?

Or . . . there was the thrush. She watched it chasing after the seeds on the counter as if they were going to run away, which, because it pecked so hard, many of them did in their way—scattering and falling off.

Birds were allowed to run errands for her, to spy for her in Grand Creek, to report back to her. It was one of the small things that Gertrude could do even with the curse—a tiny thing compared with her real power. Maybe she could send the thrush out to help Sol and Connie now. She was almost frightened to try, recalling the shadows that had formed in her shop just moments before.

She tapped the countertop hard so that the thrush looked up at her. Its eyes were black and beady, its wings brown, its belly white with black spots, its beak thin and pointy. She could have scooped it up in one hand.

"Are you ready for a big errand?" she asked it.

The thrush immediately tweeted confidently. It raised its head and pushed its belly out, singing three notes with a chatter at the end.

"I hope you can do it. And I hope you're allowed to do it. In the western valley. You birds get out there sometimes. You know who lives out there. Monique and David. You are going into their territory, and you are challenging them. You must be careful not to be seen, you understand? If they know you're helping, they'll also know where you're going."

The thrush sang a questioning melody.

"The mountain farther west and north—beyond there are the snow gentians. You must have been shown that field. Where Lenore and Fauntleroy were, long ago. That's where you must bring them, if you find them. The two children. Sol and Connie."

The thrush called out confidently again.

"You don't have to go," Gertrude said. "It's a dangerous errand." But, Gertrude thought, you're asking it to.

The thrush seemed willing.

It doesn't know just how hard this will be, Gertrude thought. Or that it might not come back. She went to the front door, opened it, and made a waving motion. The thrush leaped off the counter, flew past her, and fluttered into the street. It darted out of sight over the eaves of the opposite shop.

"*Viel Glück, kleiner Vogel*," she called out. *Lots of luck.*

No shadows rose in her shop or in the street. Gertrude was relieved. Part of her curse, then, was lifted. Now she had to figure out how much. She glanced up. The sky was gray. A storm was coming.

It was time to look for Lenore's letter. She went back into her shop and walked past the dogs, who still lay there near the back. Two of them raised their heads as she passed. Two were sleeping, their chests rising and falling. None of them got up. Apparently they knew she wasn't taking them out again or feeding them. So even the most loyal of dogs watch out first for what's most important.

She returned to the back-door landing where there were stairs up and down. Right now she chose the stairs that led up to her bedroom over the shop, but she'd use both in the end.

THE CLIMB TO THE LEDGE

THE THRUSH HAD HIGH HOPES as it flew over the colorful roofs of Grand Creek. *It* had been chosen by the All Creatures manager, among all the animals, to lead the children where they had to go. Great trust had been laid on it, although it was only a little thrush. I can do it, it thought as it flew. I'm the hero of an adventure.

It reached the creek that flowed through the willow trees, under a bridge, and past grander, older oaks. The bird tried to remember everything it had been taught about the western valley past the mountains. When it had been very young, its family had shown it the valley. They'd taken it on tours of all the streams, flowers, fields, and the thick woods that grew along the mountainsides. Still, the thrush had only the vaguest memory of those times. It had spent most of its life in town, rarely flying beyond the creek.

Now it stopped on the bank by the water. The thrush had a long journey to the mountains. A full meal was important before great tasks. It spent some time hunting along the creek for insects. Many hid under wet wood in fallen branches by the water's side. It had to wait a long time for them to poke their heads out of holes, or it had to run after insects on the move, sometimes losing one at the last moment when it lunged. The thrush wasted more time than it meant to as the clouds thickened overhead, the afternoon light faded, and the animals by the creek began their usual dusk activities.

Finally, a little hungry still, it fluttered into the forest west of town. The wind gusted, growing ever stormier. The thrush flew from branch to branch and darted over the old NO TRESPASSING sign, heading toward the mountains.

SOL'S and Connie's shouts broke the peace of the woods.

"We're he-e-re!"

"Don't go-o-o!"

Some birds took off into the air. But the woods were a big place, and their shouts seemed not to travel so far. The wind, too, swept Sol's and Connie's cries in one direction along the hill. Finally, they stopped.

"Okay, we have to stay calm," Sol said. He looked at Connie. "Are you calm?"

"I'm calm, Sol."

They stood there.

"What next?" Connie asked after a while.

"Up there, see that?"

He pointed through the treetops. Not too far away uphill, a rock ledge could be seen against the sky.

"If we could get out on that," Sol said, "we might be able to see the road. We'd have a view over the trees."

Sol started off at once through the high grass around the dark pond. Connie followed him. It was very muddy. Sol didn't say anything, but he was thinking how they were lost now because Connie had ruined his cube. And, to tell the truth, he was imagining a future that didn't include Connie—how, once they got to Aunt Heather's, maybe he'd leave Connie there and go to a boarding school. He could win a scholarship. Then he'd be alone. He could prove himself to his classmates. Somewhere Connie wouldn't ruin things for him like she sometimes did.

Did Sol often mess things up for himself? Sure, and he knew it, but that wasn't what Sol's mind was focused on at that moment.

Connie got stuck in the mud behind him and called, "I'm sinking! I'm sinking!"

Sol had to walk back to pull her out.

"You're not sinking, Connie," he said.

"I was," she answered.

They climbed uphill, trying to keep the ledge in sight. They reached places that were impassable, with too many fallen trees or prickly bushes that blocked the way. Then they had to go around. They came to a sudden drop in the land—a gully overgrown by plants spanning it from one side to the other. They had to cross it. Connie followed Sol, sliding down the side. They put their feet on tree roots for holds. Sol stumbled several times and fell once on his back.

Connie, seeing where Sol had trouble, was able to pick a better route down. Her lips tightened, and her eyes wandered as she did—as if she, like Sol, was mulling something over that she wasn't saying aloud. And she was. She was thinking about the secret that, earlier, she had decided to tell Sol.

Maybe, she thought, that wouldn't be such a good idea after all.

Sol was clambering up the other side of the gully. His arms were seriously scratched, and leaves pushed into his face whenever he grabbed a branch to hold on to. He scrambled over the edge, pulling himself up with brute force, as much as he had, then lying on his belly and swinging his legs up. He reached down and helped Connie.

The crows were gone. Sol heard them cawing at a distance. He noticed a blue and white bird stick its head into a tree knothole. What species was that? It was eating something, which made Sol hungry—or realize that he was already hungry.

After a few minutes of hiking, he finally unzipped his knapsack and pulled out his bag of potato chips. Connie did the same when she saw him take out his.

Sol had been afraid of that. Now, after they ate, they would have no food. But one small bag of chips wasn't enough for them to share, and they had to eat sometime. Sol ate while Connie struggled to open her bag, which all at once popped totally open. All the chips fell to the ground. Sol stopped and helped her pick them up. Connie blew on each a little before eating it. She had to leave a few where they lay. They were too dirty.

Sol gave her a couple of his. He took out the water bottle too and had a sip. He handed it to Connie.

She drank and handed it back to him.

There were only a few sips left.

"I'm thirsty," Connie said.

"Me too," Sol said. "The chips made us thirsty. Let's wait, though."

He put the cap on, but kept the bottle in his hand as they walked, banging it against his leg. It made a low sound. They came to a stream. They had crossed several already. This one burbled quietly, a whispering sound, as it spilled down over whitish rocks.

Sol stopped.

"Can we drink from that?" Connie asked, as if reading his mind.

"Maybe, if we have to. Before people used filters or pills to clean water, they drank from streams all the time. They lived beside them. If I remember right, the higher you are, the more away from houses and farms, the better. Also, if the water is cold. And it has to be fast-running and clear."

Sol knew a lot about water sources, underground rivers, wells, and pollution. He'd read several books on the subject. Of course, he didn't know anything about burbling streams, ancient spells or potions. He put his finger in the water. It was icy cold.

"It's probably safe. Only a tiny chance of"—he tried to remember the word and did—"cryptosporidiosis."

He went through once more, in his mind, what he knew about drinking water. Definitely no still water or slow-moving water, no water with algae, no pond water. But even fresh-looking mountain water could make you sick if you were unlucky. He felt the water in the stream. Very cold. Fast-running. Clear. He made his decision—his job as the oldest. This was as good a place as any to fill the bottle. It was getting late and, though he didn't mention it to Connie, they would have to find a place to camp soon if they didn't find the road. Unfortunately, it looked like it might rain too.

He took a sip from the bottle. He handed it to Connie.

"You can finish it," he said.

She drank the last bit and gave it back to him. Then he pushed the bottle under the surface of the stream. The water felt icy on his hand. Once the bubbles stopped sounding, he pulled it out. It was mostly full. He put it down beside him, kneeled, and leaned over the stream, cupping his hands.

He licked his lips.

He considered it.

"Only one of us should drink first," he said to Connie. "Just in case. If we both got sick, we'd be in serious trouble." He sat back without drinking. "And—there's still time. We might find the road yet."

He put the cap back on the water bottle and stood.

"Come on," he said. "Let's keep going."

They climbed farther, up something like stony

steps, although the stones were a natural part of the hill. Then, finally, they reached the start of the ledge—a rocky shelf that ran out from the hill until it was over the treetops. Sol stepped onto it. As he walked, it was very windy, so much that he decided to sit and edge himself out. Being brave didn't mean being stupid. Connie did the same. They pushed themselves, sitting and sliding, until they were far out on the ledge, the wind blowing against them. The view was impressive.

They were high up, looking over a valley half shut in by clouds. A river ran below—a snaking thread between the trees and fields. In some places were clearings, stony ridges, and hills. On their side and across the river, mountains rose, forming a ring around the valley. Many of the peaks were hidden by gray clouds that seemed to be always gathering into more. The blue sky appeared only behind torn parts of the clouds. One low peak, curved a little like a crescent moon, rose far off into the last patch of blue sky.

They saw no road.

It might be beyond the curve of the valley, Sol thought, or hidden behind hills and trees.

One thing was very interesting and surprising, though. Not far from where they sat, across the slope a little and down, was a rocky hill like a giant's bald head, and built against its side was a stone house, large and low, hidden behind high wild bushes, but easily seen from where they sat.

CHAPTER

STILL EYES

"SOMEONE LIVES HERE!" Connie said.

"Or it might be abandoned. It looks very old."

"They might help us."

"Or they might not. Whatever we do, I think we should get out of sight."

They pulled themselves back off the ledge on their behinds, the wind buffeting them. Then it was time for a decision. They had a long conversation sitting against a tree. Their final decision was to sneak carefully down to the low stone house and peer inside.

As they walked, trying to make as little noise as possible, Connie realized how loud they had been before. She heard animals scrabbling in the brush near and farther away. She listened to the wind in the trees. Often Connie or Sol stepped on a twig or shook a bush without meaning to. Once they came to a small winding brook. They jumped over it quietly.

It was a long time before they came in view of the low stone lodge, which was indeed hidden from sight in the woods unless one knew where to look.

"You stay here," Sol said.

Connie pushed her lips to one side in a half frown. She was starting to get annoyed at Sol with his "I have to take care of you" talk. Still, she had to admit, it was up to the older of them to take the risk now. Connie would have to wait and do something heroic only if events called for it.

Sol was already on his way, sneaking around the side of the lodge, although Connie heard him even after he disappeared from her sight. He was no Boy Scout. Her thoughts turned again to her secret, about the Valentine's Day card that Sol had packed. Her secret was that *she* had made the card, not another girl. Connie clearly remembered the day last year—in February. Her teacher, Ms. Dowell, had suggested then that the kids in Connie's class make a Valentine's Day card for their parents.

Connie had almost raised her hand that day in school and asked, "What if you don't like your parents?" There'd only been her father, Mr. Blink, plus the woman who was soon to become Connie and Sol's stepmother, who was just as mean.

But Connie knew nobody would understand her question, especially Ms. Dowell. So instead of asking, Connie had decided to make the Valentine's Day card for Sol instead. She'd been feeling in a nice mood that day. She drew bright red hearts. She could almost hear Sol saying as she did, *Real hearts don't look anything like that.* But these were the hearts she was supposed to draw. And she was doing the assignment, really, just because Ms. Dowell had asked her to.

Dear Sol, Will you be my valentine? Connie had written in the neatest handwriting she could manage. She made it especially girlie because that fit in with the card. Connie could be tricky, even in her handwriting. She had practiced forging her father's signature, for instance. Then just at the moment of signing the card—maybe because she sometimes signed things under other names, like her father's—she had written *Your Secret Valentine* instead. She thought it was more fun to be a secret valentine than just herself.

Connie had shown it to Ms. Dowell as she walked by.

"It's for my brother."

Ms. Dowell glanced at it and smiled approvingly.

"Very nice," the teacher said.

Getting into making the card more, Connie had added a pair of kissing lips in bright red near the bottom. She knew how to draw those too. This will be funny, she thought. In her mind, she figured Sol would know right away that it was from her.

Who else?

Her class ate and then had recess while Sol's class went to the cafeteria. Younger kids always ate earlier. She was able to walk by Sol's empty classroom. Most kids would never have gone into an empty classroom of the upper grades, but Connie wasn't most kids. She was fearless about such things. She had walked in. The classroom was shadowy with the lights turned off. She'd known where Sol's desk was, slipped in the valentine card, and walked out of the classroom. No one had noticed her.

And this is the part Connie had never thought of. She had been sure that Sol would come out at the end of the day saying, "Oh, if it isn't my secret valentine! I'd recognize those hearts anywhere."

But Connie hadn't realized there were actual secret

valentine cards going around Sol's class because they were older, and signed ones too. Sol's world was different from Connie's. Several boys in Sol's class had gotten cards from girls, and girls had gotten cards from boys too. Secret valentines were quickly found out. Either a friend in the class ratted, or rumors would go around until the secret admirer had to admit it.

Now, Sol was not the sort of boy ever to get a valentine. When he opened his desk after lunchtime and saw the card, Sol could hardly believe it. He kept it under his desk, opened it, read it, and glanced around to see if anyone was watching. No one was. Sol wasn't dumb, of course. He knew someone might have left the card as a joke—or a trick. But his mind immediately went to the kids in his class. If Sol showed it to any of them, he thought, whoever wrote it would announce the joke, and they would all tease him for believing that he could have gotten a real valentine.

There was another possibility, though, that Sol could think of, a more positive one. Sol had to admit the chance to himself since he was logical. Maybe he really *did* have a secret valentine. Maybe someone in his class had left it for him for real.

And Sol had a crush on one girl in particular. She

wasn't one of the most popular girls. She was a smart, practical girl. Sol had to admit, there was some possibility that it came from her. Although, life being what it was, that was definitely wishful thinking.

Still, the fact that none of the kids came over and tried to get a look at it or trick him into mentioning it or simply tear it out of his hands made him think even more that it wasn't a trick after all. If it had been one, whoever had written it would have found some way during the day to make him show the card.

Sol snuck a look at the card several times. *Will you be my valentine?* Then, when he had the best chance, he put it into his knapsack.

When Connie had met Sol at the end of the school day, she saw immediately that he was in a good mood. And, since he didn't mention the card, Connie realized at once why. Sol thought he had a real secret admirer.

Connie, then, didn't have the heart to tell him. She hadn't wanted to burst his bubble. Plus, she was just a little afraid that he would be upset with her. So that secret had joined the list of Connie's secrets from Sol, but, in all honesty, it was one of the smaller and less important ones.

She wouldn't even have thought of it again,

except that now he had packed the card, which meant it was important to him. She wondered, waiting in the woods, if it was fair to let Sol keep believing something that was false. She knew for a fact that he wanted her to admit any time that she had fooled him or done something she wasn't supposed to—like snuck into his room.

But she had never meant to fool him with the card.

And she wondered if she really was supposed to tell him everything, all the time. No, she decided. Definitely not, even if they were a team. A sister and brother don't have to tell each other everything, she thought. And it was just a small lie—just a mistake, really.

Now was definitely *not* the time to tell him.

And who knows, she thought, maybe inside this stone lodge is someone helpful, like the animal-store woman had been helpful in Grand Creek. There *were* nice people in the world. Connie could feel it. Thinking of the All Creatures manager made Connie feel calmer.

⁓⁂⁓

MEANWHILE, Sol wasn't calm at all as he snuck around the side of the stone lodge, trying to be quiet. Over the door hung a polished horn of some sort—from a ram, Sol thought. A window of thick glass was cemented into the stones. The glass was wavy, the uneven kind used long ago. It was indeed an ancient dwelling.

Sol had a feeling, as he approached, that no one was home. He wondered why he thought that, and he realized it was because there was no light coming from the window, even though it was getting toward dusk. Perhaps the home was abandoned after all. When he raised his head slowly over the windowsill to peer inside, though, he saw that wasn't true.

And his heart skipped a beat. He was looking into a room with a fireplace and a doorway into the stone hill itself—maybe to a bedroom. Animals stood everywhere inside: a black bear, two wolves, a fox, a boar, a huge caribou, weasels and rabbits, an opossum, a beaver, an armadillo, a duck. They stood in strange poses, some like they were dancing, some like they were running.

Sol had seen stuffed animals in museums, of course. He'd seen the heads of elk and moose hanging on the walls of restaurants. But this room was something else. He felt at once that no good person lived here.

The second he thought that, he felt someone might be watching him. He turned around, but no one was there. Whoever lived here might be gone for now or in that other room. His eyes fell on the spot among the trees where he knew Connie was crouched.

We've got to get away, Sol thought.

Moving fast, and making more noise than he hoped to, he reached Connie, who with one glance knew that they were leaving. Not cautiously enough, they rushed downhill. Soon they were crashing through the forest without any concern for the noise they made. It was too late to try to stay quiet.

But soon they began to feel that no one was following them. They hiked on at a regular pace for a good twenty minutes or half an hour—what seemed like a long time. Sol told Connie what he'd seen in the stone house.

"We're really in trouble, Sol, aren't we?" Connie said.

"We can make it one night in these woods," Sol answered, "if it doesn't rain. We can find our way out. Even if we don't have food, even if it takes days. What worries me is who's in here with us."

"Another witch?" Connie asked.

"Something like that," Sol said. He recalled ancient, traditional Holaderry back in Grand Creek. What were other old traditions? "One good thing," he said.

"What?"

"I didn't see any stuffed children in there."

They were silent after that.

"I'm sorry, Sol," Connie said. "*I'm* the one who got us lost."

Sol seemed surprised for a second. "It's okay, Connie. I didn't get us out of here either." He couldn't help adding, "Just . . . you know."

"What?"

"Just . . . don't get caught again. Like last time."

Now Connie was really upset.

"You make sure *you* don't get caught," she said. "And stop saying that *you* have to watch out for *me*. I can take care of myself."

"I know you can," Sol said. Although something in his tone of voice made Connie feel like he didn't totally believe it. "And don't shout," Sol added.

They fell silent again.

"Did you bring matches?" Connie asked.

Sol shook his head. "No matches, Connie. No

lighter. No flashlight. You neither?" Sol looked at her. "We thought we were safe, didn't we? When we were out of Grand Creek with Holaderry gone. Just a bus ride to safety. But—we're going to make it, Connie. We did it once. We'll do it again."

"We *will*," Connie said, trying to make herself feel better.

The forest was darkening into a single mass of curvy shadows, though the clouds still held some light above. The sun must have set past the mountains a little while before, Sol thought. He and Connie stood in an area of twisted trees. A stream wound through. One of the trees bent out on one side and in on the other, a little like a giant cobra's hood. That tree and the rising land around it would provide some shelter, Sol thought.

"It's too dark to go on," he said. "We should gather pine needles, leaves, just from nearby, and lay them here. If we get dry needles, it'll be a little softer then."

Sol couldn't believe he was suggesting they lie on a bed of leaves and pine needles on the ground and try to sleep. But there weren't any mattresses in the woods.

He and Connie managed to scrape together

handfuls of pine needles. Sol noticed, in the trees, several crows watching them, black shapes moving along the dark branches. He discovered something odd by feel under pine needles that he was collecting in one place. He examined it in the dim light. A small pocket-knife, the kind of knife a kid might have had. It was rusty, obviously dropped long ago—maybe several years. Sol tried to open it, but it was rusted shut.

"Connie, come look."

He showed it to her.

"A knife!" she said. "That's useful, Sol."

"No. It doesn't open."

"Well, but it means someone was here before us," Connie said. "Another kid, right? That's good. Maybe he's still here."

Sol shook his head. "This has been here for years."

"Well," Connie tried again, "it means that someone got lost before, and so they must have made it out, and we will too."

Sol didn't try to correct her. He knew that she knew the flaw in her logic just as well as he did.

"Let's look around, Connie. See what else we can find."

But it was really too dark to look by then. They didn't find anything else. It was growing stormier.

Soon the wind blew so strongly that the treetops waved over them. They finished making their bed of leaves and pine needles and lay down close to the wide cobra-shaped tree. They pushed against each other. Normally Sol wouldn't have slept that way—he liked to sleep alone. But it was warmer to sleep together, that was a scientific fact. And, less scientifically, it made him feel better to have an arm against Connie.

They lay a long time, talking a little. Connie managed to fall asleep, even snoring. Sol couldn't sleep, though. He listened to the wind in the trees, dying down, then gusting. He worried about rain. Also, every time he shut his eyes, he saw in his mind that elk staring at him, then the room in the stone lodge, full of animals. Some of those animals had stared at him too—as he'd peered through the window—with their still eyes.

Suddenly he remembered Holaderry's journal, which he was carrying with them. He should have thought of it much earlier. Maybe it had something about the woods here. He sat up and reached for his knapsack, just a dark shape beside him. He unzipped it quietly. He found the witch's journal inside by the feel of its smooth leather cover, and pulled it out.

He paged through it. But Holaderry had written

in black ink, the pages were gray, and it was just too dark to read. There was no moon. He squinted and turned a few pages. Then he closed the journal again. Oh well, he thought. He put it back into his knapsack. When he did, he felt the water bottle in there. Sol was very thirsty. He would have to drink in the morning anyway and all day tomorrow, he thought. And it was important, just like he'd told Connie, that he test it first.

So he pulled the bottle out, unscrewed the cap by feel, took some sips, screwed the cap back on, and laid the bottle beside him. He closed his eyes and tried to sleep.

Connie had stopped snoring. She rolled over and said sleepily, "Sol?"

"I'm here," Sol said softly.

There was a pause.

"I'm sorry I ruined your cube," Connie said.

"Don't worry about it. It's not important."

"Are you mad at me?"

Sol didn't answer for a long time.

"No," he said finally.

"I don't believe you."

"Connie, try to get some sleep."

"It's not very comfortable. I've got a root sticking into me."

"Then roll over."

She didn't.

"Do you think there'll be someone here, Sol," she asked in the darkness, "to help us? Like the animal woman in Grand Creek?"

"I don't know, Connie," Sol said. "But whatever happens, we'll help each other."

CHAPTER

THE FIRST NIGHT

AFTER GOING to her bedroom and finding Lenore's letter in her closet, Gertrude had gone down both flights of stairs to the cool cellar underneath her shop. Her cellar's central room was for normal things—storing extra boxes of the pet and animal products she sold. The back cellar room, though, wasn't so normal. It held bookcases reaching the low ceiling. Almost all the books were exactly the same height and the same color—dusty red.

What kind of library was this where the books all looked the same? It was a legal library. Those books explained laws and trial judgments, but not from any town, state, or national government. Instead, they described the supernatural laws and judgments of witches and other evil creatures.

Before taking down any of the books, Gertrude first sat at the small round table in the cellar library and read through Lenore's letter, written in a girlish hand on thick, darkened paper centuries old. It was just as Gertrude remembered it. Sent to her from far away with no return address, stamped in a northern territory that was gigantic. Lenore had never wanted to be found again. She had lost what was most important to her, but she had escaped, and she'd wanted after that only to lead a good, quiet life, away from the struggles of the world. Back then, there had been places to go where a girl like Lenore could disappear.

I hope you found peace in the end, Gertrude thought as she reread the letter. I'm sorry you lost what you did.

The details of the letter would be useful later. And she was glad to see that her memory had been correct about the field of snow gentians and the cave.

But now she needed to know something more, that she could discover only in her legal books: What might she be allowed to do since the object of her curse—her cane—had been returned to her, but not the whole thing?

There are emergencies that call for quick action, fast talking, or heroic feats. But for Gertrude this emergency meant reading all night by the lone bulb that hung over the table.

She searched through the dusty tomes on her shelves, sticking torn paper in places for bookmarks, stacking useless books to the side. She grew so tired and frustrated that once she tried to use her powers again without knowing how far she might take them. And once more, dark forces rose around her, spinning in a closing circle that made even Gertrude's experienced heart pound. She had to stop and she dared not try again—not even one time—until she understood the half curse that still held her.

As she read on, her thoughts sometimes wandered. She knew in her heart that the little thrush hadn't reached Sol and Connie yet, and she admitted to herself that it might never do so. Her mind turned then to exactly the question that Connie had asked Sol that night.

Might there be someone in the mountains who would help Sol and Connie the way she had helped them in Grand Creek and was trying to help them now? But as far as Gertrude knew, there was no one like that there.

✦

THE thrush, meanwhile, hadn't even reached the first peak before the valley. Gale-force winds mounted in the forest west of Grand Creek as if on purpose to delay the bird. Though not even the witch of the woods could call up such a storm. Still, no matter how or why, that night the gusts bent treetops and took hold of the thrush—sent it flailing against branches. Once, the thrush was thrown to the ground so forcefully it injured its right wing. Then it felt pain when it flew onward.

Yet the thrush struggled on. It would do what was asked of it. It would find strength and defeat this evil wind! But even as it tried, a gust picked it up and threw it spinning through the air as if it were a paper ball. It landed on a branch, hanging on with its claws as the branch waved and shook. It waited for a lull and launched forward again.

So it flew for one hour, two hours, three hours, and more. The thrush was still very far from the accursed valley. As the night passed, it lost all its optimism. It had been so confident when it had first set off. Now it flew according to what the storm would allow, even going in the wrong direction occasionally if it had to.

The thrush felt regret then that *it*, of all creatures, had been chosen and trusted with such an important errand.

⁓✦⁓

SOME distance from where Sol and Connie slept, a light was flickering in the woods, and the crackling pop of a campfire could be heard whenever the wind died down. A woman was sitting on a tree stump before that fire, staring into its flames. She looked young—or not too old. She wore a camping shirt with four pockets, tan pants, hiking boots, and a green cap. Her hair was tied back in a ponytail. On her belt she wore three large pouches, like sacks, and out from one of these poked branches. In a pile near her, lit by the flickering firelight, lay more berry branches and fresh leaves.

She leaned toward the fire, her elbows on her knees. She held a twig in her hand that she twirled for a while, then tossed into the flames. She picked up another twig and began to twirl that. On the grass beside her sat a different kind of bag than the ones on her belt, a little one which she had found hanging from a branch. A bit of bark and black fur stuck out of it.

She glanced every once in a while into the woods—as if she could see right through them—toward where Sol and Connie slept.

CHAPTER

THE HUNTER'S CURSE

FROM DAVID BITTWORTH'S LOG:

IF YOU ASK ME who is to blame for my curse, on nine out of ten dark nights as I sit in this stone lodge, I will tell you that Monique, the witch of these woods, the queen of this accursed valley, is to blame. On the tenth night, though, I might tell you the truth.

I am to blame.

I hate to admit it. As I told you, I never wanted to be a villain. But what we want to be and who we are, those are two different things. The hard truth is I cursed myself by riding into this valley, by leading my friends in the hunt.

Others warned me.

"Stay out of there," they told me. "It's evil."

I even met an old woman who read my fortune with cards, who shrieked and cackled, her eyes reflecting the flame of her candle. She raised her wrinkled arms and screamed at me, "Go not into the accursed woods!"

I laughed and gave her the coin she was due. After that, I might have been the tiniest bit scared when I rode into this valley. But each time my hunting party and I returned unharmed, loaded down with animals of the most impressive sort, I grew less worried. We held feasts. We roasted deer, elk, even bear, and I presented the mayor of our town with gifts from the hunt—felled animals.

My friends and I were spoken of as fearless. We had ridden into the accursed valley and come back, after all. I loved it, how the townspeople looked at me. Let me tell you, when others look at you with awe and admiration in their eyes, it is only natural to think, There must be something to it. I AM special.

We never mentioned that the accursed valley was actually a hunter's paradise, full of animals. We never explained how easy it was to ride in and out, that nothing blocked our way. Instead we told everyone just the opposite. We recounted stories of how scary and strange it was in the valley.

"The mountain peaks," we told them, "are like evil spirits watching you. The trees moan in the breeze with the voices of ghosts. The witch's laughter can be heard in the pattering of drops when it rains."

The truth was that I never heard nor saw a ghost or witch or monster or anything frightening in the valley at all. It never occurred to me, of course, that WE were the monsters, that we were the thing for others to fear— for unlucky children to fear, the children who disappeared in the woods and were never heard from again.

Now I understand that I was like a boy proud to beat an adult at a game, fully unaware that he's been allowed to win. There comes a time, though, when a child like that learns he's being toyed with. That day came to me too, when I learned that the witch was toying with us, turning the lost children into animals whom we hunted and brought back for our feasts.

I wasn't a winner after all.

I learned it for sure on a clear autumn day when I led my party into the accursed valley. I remember it well. My friends who rode with me always joked and called me "the king," since I was the best hunter among us and their leader.

They did the same that day. "What say you, king?"

they asked me, laughing astride their horses. And, "Your orders, sire?" They bowed their heads.

I played along as usual.

"Today we hunt," I told them. "Tonight we feast!"

"Hurrah!" they cried.

We blew our hunting horns, and we rode. I spotted a young deer, half hidden by brush. The chase was on. I left my friends behind. The deer ran as fast as it could, but I kept up easily. Its stride was nothing compared to my horse's. The deer splashed across a brook and, in its confusion, chose just the wrong path, ending up trapped near the edge of a high cliff. I drew my arrow from its quiver in a split second, aimed, and let the arrow fly.

Now, you would no doubt like to hear that something in this deer's gaze, as it turned back to look at me, made me avert my shot. But the truth is, I think, I was simply worried that if my arrow struck the deer wrong, the deer might fall over the cliff's edge and I would lose it completely.

The deer leaped toward me as I shot, a little crookedly, and my arrow struck its leg.

It ran off, back in the direction we'd come from. I gave chase through the brook, and there, where I'd first spotted the young deer, I noticed something tangled in the bushes. A red ribbon. I slowed, stopped, and rode back. I leaned over from my horse to pluck the ribbon off, and I studied it. It was woven of a fine fabric. Sewn into the ribbon were initials: LG.

It must have come from the deer, I realized.

It was a signal in those days to tie a ribbon to a wild animal if it wasn't truly wild, if it belonged to someone—a farmer who fed it or a family that had found the animal and nursed it back to health. They would tie a ribbon to the animal to show that it was not to be hunted.

There were no farms or families in this accursed valley, though. That much I knew.

And it was no fault of mine to have hunted the deer if I hadn't seen the ribbon, I thought to myself. I put it in my vest pocket and went in search of the deer, then, to finish it off. It was cruel to leave an animal wounded from a poorly aimed shot. That was the rule when hunting. You had to end what you started. So I reasoned to myself, ribbon or no ribbon.

But even as I rode on, I began to feel the curse of the valley hanging heavy over me. I had always ignored that feeling before—the feeling that I was somehow tied to the accursed valley and that each time I came to hunt here and returned home with more prizes, the curse was tightening around me like a lasso. I felt it like a secret that must never be told, not even to myself.

I knew there was something wrong with what we were doing, you see, even if I refused to think carefully about why. I had pushed aside every thought of what might be happening to the children who came into this valley and never came out. I always believed that if I was cursed, it would mean something bad happened TO me. I refused to consider that the curse of this valley, at least for me, might be the opposite—something bad that I did to others.

The deer's trail led me to a small stone hut we ourselves had built earlier, for protection against bad weather during our hunts. In front of the hut lay the wounded deer. A girl was tending to its wound, bent over it on her knees. She was a big girl, dressed in fine but ruined traveling clothes. She had torn off one of her sleeves as a bandage to cover where my arrow went in. And she'd broken off the arrow too, but hadn't pulled it out. She knew something, then, about tending to wounds. She looked up at me on my horse. I will never forget that look.

"What are you doing here?" I shouted at her. "Don't you know these woods are accursed?"

She nodded. "We're runaways. This was the one route that no one would suspect we were on."

"We?" I asked. "You and your pet deer?"

"He's no pet," she said. "He is my brother. He's but five years of age. He drank from a stream in these woods, and it poisoned him. Enchanted him. Changed him to what you see now. I tied one of my ribbons around his neck, but it must have fallen off. He grew frightened when he heard the hunting horns, and he bolted from me."

Normally I would have called the girl mad, claiming an animal for her brother. The wounded deer, after all, had not one human thing about it. It looked like a true deer. But the way the girl touched it and looked into its black eyes, I knew that she was telling the truth.

And that is when I understood that I was cursed.

"And you?" she asked. "Why are you here?"

I glanced at the hunting horn on my belt. I felt the weight of the bow on my shoulder. I noticed the red ribbon poking out from my pocket, though she didn't seem to see it. I quickly stuffed it down. I made a decision.

"Why, I and my friends have ridden into these woods to rescue you and him," I lied. "Come, get up behind me. I will ride you out."

"And my brother?"

"He can trot beside us. I have seen deer run very far with worse injuries." I didn't say how I had seen such things.

She took my hand. I was thankful that she did. I pulled her up to the saddle behind me and started off. I blew my horn three times, the signal for our hunting party to meet. They came in ones and twos, catching up to us as we rode. There were seven of them. My seven friends.

Once all of them were assembled and riding with me, I stopped us and told them, "I found the children." They stared at me, wondering what I was talking about. "The children we've been looking for. To rescue!" I went on, with meaning in my voice. "It's as we suspected, the boy here has been enchanted by the witch of the woods and turned into a simple beast. And . . . somewhere in these woods are hunters like us, but very mean, bad, terrible ones."

"David," my closest friend, Karl, asked, "won't the witch be upset if we ride the children out?"

I gave Karl a stern look.

"Who am I?" I asked, turning to them all.

"You're the king," my friends answered.

"Exactly. Then you have my command. Follow me!"

And though I saw they were frightened of the witch of the woods, the queen of this accursed valley, that we were challenging her, they did as I said. We rode.

We had to go slowly at first, because the deer was hurt much worse than I had imagined. Eventually I stopped, dismounted, and lifted the animal—a terrific feat of strength—to lay it on my horse's back. I secured the brother with rope, just as I would have done with game I'd felled. Freed from his slow speed, then we galloped through the forest, the girl clutching me from behind.

Every minute that we defied the curse of the valley was a minute that brought out the valley's true nature more. When we had been a part of its evil plan, the woods had looked normal to us, even pretty. Now, though, the branches of the trees took on fearful shapes, faces staring from them. My horse slowed too, as if fighting against a current.

And SHE rose before us, as we crossed a great field. She was just a shadow with a voice, a darkness that hung in the air. She wouldn't let us see her that day, although now I can. Her shadow started off human sized, but soon it grew until it was as tall as the trees—a black cloud before us—and spread overhead into the sky like it might fall upon us and swallow us up.

"I should have known," I whispered to myself.

She heard.

"You knew!" Monique's voice spoke from one place and then another in the shadow. "You all knew. You hunted here with my permission because I wanted it. You were allowed in as hunters because the valley wants it. You cannot defy us now. It's too late for you. But I give you one chance still. Leave the children behind. Then you may ride out of these mountains and never look back. Else . . ."

She didn't say else what. I often ask myself what I would have done if I'd known the answer to that question.

"Ride on, men!" I called out.

But my party didn't answer. There was no sound at all from behind. When I spun my horse round, I saw why. They were frozen in place like statues.

I was stronger, though. I'd been the best of them, the king, they'd called me, and I was still the best. I kicked my horse hard with my sharp spurs. My horse obeyed the pain and started off. The sister gripped me from behind.

I still remember that ride. For that one short ride, I was a good man.

We got very far up into the mountains, so hard did I strain, and my horse too. The mountain pass was ahead, the nearest one. I sensed that the witch's power would end at that mountaintop. The other side of the mountain was a different valley.

But finally my horse slowed to a trot, then a walk. Then it stopped.

"You must get off here," I told the girl. "I won't be able to go farther. But you can."

I dismounted and helped her down. I untied the deer and half pulled, half lifted it off. It stood shakily on its legs. It was badly hurt, and the ride had pulled the wound wide open.

The girl walked away with her brother the deer, without so much as a goodbye.

I guess she knew what had really happened. That it was the tip of my own arrow that was stuck in her brother's leg. And yet she had also trusted me when I'd offered help.

The deer limped by her side. She kept her hand on him as she led him up past the trees to the stony mountaintop.

I felt like I could take no step closer to that mountain pass, no step closer to freedom.

I wandered back down through the woods, leading my horse by its reins much as the girl had led her brother, except we were going to imprisonment instead of to freedom. We haven't left the valley since.

I found Monique, or she found me. She let me see her then. What a sight!

"Are you ready to face your fate?" she asked me.

I shook my head.

"No," I told her, "I'm not."

CHAPTER

12

HEADACHE AND FEVER

SOL DIDN'T FEEL WELL when he woke. He'd had bad dreams, but he couldn't remember them. His head throbbed with pain. He saw rain clouds in the morning sky through the trees. He heard birds calling all around. It was very early. The bird calls sounded loud and clear. Even through his headache he could tell exactly where each bird was. He smelled the morning too—he almost tasted it in his dry mouth.

He turned to look for Connie, which made his headache throb worse.

"Connie, wake up," he said.

Connie opened her sleepy eyes to look at him. As sleep left her, Connie's expression changed.

"Are you okay?" she asked, sitting up.

"I don't feel good."

"You don't look good," she said.

"Feel my forehead, Connie."

She put her palm on his head, almost at once scrunching her cheeks up.

"You're all sweaty." She took her hand off.

"And hot?" he asked.

Connie nodded. "You're sick, Sol." She said it loudly or it sounded that way to him.

He half closed his eyes at the pain and breathed out slowly.

"It's the water, Connie," he said quietly. "It must be. I drank it last night. You didn't drink any?"

"No, Sol. I just woke up."

"Good." Despite his pain he was glad. "Pour it out," he said.

He turned his head slowly and saw the bottle lying very close to him. He reached his arm out and took it. Oddly, he found it hard to bend his fingers. He handed it to her.

Connie walked over to the stream. She uncapped the bottle, turned it upside down, and let the water pour out. It made a loud *glug-glug* sound. She held the bottle as far from her as she could, as if just the touch of the water might hurt her. She shook it to get the last drops out.

"Keep it," Sol said. "Keep the bottle. We don't have anything else for water."

Connie made a face like she didn't agree. But she packed the water bottle in Sol's knapsack.

He put his arm across his eyes. Then he lowered the arm and used it to push himself up to a sitting position. At once, he coughed as if he might vomit. His stomach heaved. He leaned over. But he didn't vomit.

He regained a little strength. He closed his eyes again, focusing on his head. He breathed deeply, slowly, in and out. He put a hand on the ground.

"Help me up," he said.

Connie took his arm. Pushing off her, he was able to stand. But he immediately felt bad. He put his hands on his thighs and leaned over, breathing deeply, until he finally steadied himself, only slightly bent forward.

Connie thought he seemed a little taller than usual.

"How do you feel, Sol?"

"Okay." He closed his eyes for a second. "Not too good. My head feels like two poles are stuck into it, and my stomach is like I ate—I don't know—something bad. I feel really cold too. And my skin, it's tingling all over."

He stopped talking. He was bent halfway over again. He wavered, reached out, and leaned against a tree.

"What should I do, Sol?"

Sol didn't answer. He had put his head against the tree, so that he was pushing his forehead into its bark. The branches were waving in the wind. Connie looked up. The weather looked bad, like rain.

Connie realized at once that, even though she complained a lot about how Sol should treat her equally even if she was younger, she didn't like having the weight of responsibility on her shoulders now, lost in the woods at dawn.

What to do? she asked silently to herself this time.

Away from the stream, she thought. It wasn't the same one Sol had filled the bottle from, but this little winding stream through the twisted trees could be poisoned too, maybe on purpose. Sol might be sick from drinking from a stream with things growing in it. But Connie didn't think so. She thought there was almost certainly magic or a witch at work.

"Can you walk?" Connie asked Sol quietly.

This time he answered, to Connie's great relief.

"I think so."

"Come on," Connie said.

She put his knapsack on him, put her own on, and led him in the easiest direction away from the stream, through pine trees spaced far enough apart to walk between. Pine needles carpeted the ground. After a few minutes, they came into a clearing with a big circular mound, black and white, in the wild grass.

Connie went to look. It was the leftovers from a fire. Blackened wood and white ash. She looked around the clearing but could find no other clues as to who had been there.

She led Sol onward. She took them downhill whenever possible, away from the closest mountain. It was easier for Sol to go downhill. He was in bad shape, stumbling along. The going wasn't easy, because every slope down reached a turning point—a low point—and then they had to climb up. Sol sighed a lot. He took steps, then leaned over and coughed. He walked into a thicket without thinking—fell against it and seemed almost glad to be leaning into the tangled thin branches, which gave under him and supported him. Resting.

"Let's sit for a minute," Sol said.

He crouched then and there, leaning on his arm and sitting, even though it wasn't a comfortable place to sit at all—overgrown with high grass that had pointy white stuff growing along its blades.

He breathed in and out loudly. He lay back at once on top of his bumpy knapsack, putting his arm across his forehead. Soon he was sleeping—or lying there still—his knees bent up, his shirt rising and falling visibly as he breathed, tall wild grass sticking into him, and he didn't seem to care.

Connie didn't know what to do. The wind had died down some time ago, but the clouds were dark overhead. She was the one who had to make decisions now. She called Sol's name, but he didn't move. She looked up and saw a crow staring at her from a branch. She didn't feel that the crow was evil. But that didn't mean it was nice either. It looked like it didn't care what happened here in these woods.

"Why don't you do something?" she shouted at the crow. But it just leaped to another branch and cawed, and three more joined it. Others wheeled overhead. Connie heard another bird cry, off in the distance. Closer, a bird sang a two-note melody— low-high, low-high.

"Help," Connie said, almost quietly. "Help-help," she called out like the bird call.

Shortly after, she heard movements. The rustling of bushes, the not-so-loud cracking of pine needles underfoot. Like a large animal, but one that knew how to move quietly when it wanted to. She thought of the elk. She wouldn't have minded seeing it then.

But it wasn't the elk.

There was movement in the forest. Connie saw it out of the corner of her eye. But when she turned to look, it was gone. No, wait, it was there, something moving between the trees.

"Someone's there," Connie said softly, although Sol didn't seem to hear her.

A woman stepped into the clearing. She was young—not very young, but not too old either. She had pouches hanging from her belt and held a branch in her hand with berries on it. She wore a camping shirt, tan pants, hiking boots, and a green cap. Her hair was tied back in a ponytail.

"I was afraid of this," she said, speaking very

quietly. She came up to Connie. Her glance fell on Sol lying in the tall grass.

"Are you hurt?" she asked Connie. She put a hand on Connie's shoulder and looked, concerned, into Connie's eyes. Next she turned her attention to Sol.

"He drank from a stream?" she whispered.

Connie nodded. "Who are you?" she asked.

"Let's just say that I'm a friend," the woman said quietly. "You called for help, thank God. So now I can help you. You didn't drink from the stream?"

"No," Connie said, talking almost in a whisper too now, like the woman.

The woman looked surprised.

"That's very lucky. And I'll tell you what else is lucky." She lifted a small bag from her belt, different from the big pouches that she wore. "This. I found this. *She* dropped it. And it means we might have a chance."

She crouched and picked up Sol's hands, examining them. Sol turned his head to the side as if trying to sleep. She loosened his sneakers and pulled them off, then his socks, and checked his feet.

"He hasn't turned much yet."

She pulled up Sol's shirt. Sol had long whitish hair growing on his chest, all in the same direction, downward.

Connie was very surprised.

The woman rolled up his short sleeves, and he had the same hair growing on his shoulders but browner. She felt Sol's forehead, running her fingertips over it.

"Here. Feel this."

She took Connie's hand and put it on Sol's head. Connie felt that it was hot with fever, but that wasn't what the woman was talking about. There were two bumps on Sol's forehead, like the bumps that swell up when one hits one's head hard.

"What are they?" Connie asked.

"Later." She stood. "We don't have much time. When did he drink exactly?"

"Last night."

The woman kept her eyes on Connie, but her mind seemed to go elsewhere.

"Okay. Look, she made a big mistake dropping that bag. Finally. You've got a chance now. The transformation won't be complete until she figures out some way to get the last ingredients into him. And she's lost the element of surprise. I might be able to turn this back."

Quickly she put Sol's socks and sneakers back on. She placed her hands under Sol's arms, lifted him— "Ups-a-daisy," she said quietly—and laid him over her shoulder, her hand on his legs to hold him.

To Connie she said, "Follow me."

CHAPTER

13

THE CAMPER LADY

CONNIE HURRIED AFTER the woman—whom she thought of as the Camper Lady. That woman followed a trail only she could see, but a trail it was, the type that larger animals in the woods use. However narrow or overgrown it looked, there was always a path through.

Rain started. Connie heard it as drops against the leaves before she felt it. They crested a hill and emerged in sight of a huge, rushing brook. The brook, while not exactly raging, splashed loudly against boulders—its sound mixing with the sound of the rain—as it fell toward a river that could be seen through the trees downslope.

The woman, carrying Sol, stepped confidently but carefully in the rain across the brook from boulder to boulder, jumping in places onto slippery-looking rocks that just broke the rushing water's surface. She looked back when she reached the other side.

Connie hadn't crossed. She was just standing there in the rain. "I don't think I can get across," she called.

The woman put Sol down, laying him gently on the ground on his back, supporting his head as she did. Then she came easily across the brook and picked Connie up by the armpits. She grabbed Connie's upper legs and lay Connie over her shoulder just the way she had been carrying Sol.

"Hold still," she said. Connie, upside down, staring down the woman's back, took hold of the woman's shirt while trying to keep her arms up enough to hold her knapsack from slipping off her shoulders. It still slipped and hung over her head from her arms. She had to hold it up, using her strength, while the Camper Lady's shoulder jutted into Connie's belly and they jumped from boulder to boulder.

They reached the other side, and the Camper Lady let Connie down. Then she hoisted Sol without a moment's delay and continued on her way, keeping the river at a distance but not moving away from it either.

So they came to a large cabin built of huge, long old logs with a new log—standing out because of its lighter, less weather-beaten color—here and there along the side. Over the door hung a homemade wreath, and it was under this wreath they passed to enter the cabin, which was warm from a burning woodstove. The woman closed the door quickly but gently; as she pushed it the final inch, it squeaked. She latched it shut.

Then she laid Sol down on the only bed in the cabin, a cot with a patchwork quilt. The rain drummed on the roof. She pushed the quilt aside to lay him down.

"Actually, we should get him into dry clothes. Do you have some in his pack?"

Connie nodded.

"You do it, okay? Change his pants and, well, take his shirt off and leave it off. We need to watch him, and I need to treat him. No socks either. I'll keep him warm."

She went over to the woodstove, opened the door in front—Connie saw the glow of embers—put in a split log, and shut the door again. The woodstove was an iron-colored box on legs with a flat top wide enough for two pots. One tall pot of steaming water stood on it now.

A metal chimney, like a wide pipe, ran from the back top of the stove, across the cabin wall, and then out. Behind the pipe along the wall hung woven blankets with scenes of nature on them—one devoted to different types of trees growing through each other, another showing what might have been a summer field.

While the woman occupied herself with the stove and the two cabin windows—no glass, just solid wooden shutters—Connie pulled Sol's other pants out of his knapsack, which was wet on the outside but mostly dry inside. She then spent a lot of time and energy tugging his wet pants off, getting his legs through the new pants, and pulling their waist up to just below his behind. She had to lift his behind up to get the pants on.

"Do you need help?" the woman asked without looking over, propping open a shutter just a little, letting in fresh air and the rushing sound of the rain.

"No, I've got it." Connie leaned close to Sol's ear. "Come on, Sol, lift up a bit so I can get your pants on."

He seemed to hear and, even though he kept his eyes closed, he pushed his feet so that his middle lifted a bit, letting out a soft whimper through closed lips. Connie pulled the pants up. They seemed too narrow at the hips and stretched out. When she tried to button them, the button didn't reach.

Next she pulled his shirt up and gasped in shock as she saw his chest. It was covered in the fine, almost white hairs she had seen before, all the way up to his shoulders and down close to his belly button. She pulled the shirt totally off, whispering again to Sol to get him to raise his arms. He smelled terrible under his armpits where he'd been sweating. Putting his shirt to the side, she touched the hairs. They were soft. She stroked them.

"He's changing." The woman had come up behind her. "I don't know. We might be too late to turn it all the way back. But—don't worry, I'll try. I've got a few tricks of my own."

She laid a hand on Sol's forehead. The bumps had grown, and skin flaked off in large pieces. Under the peeling skin, the bumps were off-white—the color of teeth—hardened and smooth. Like what? Connie knew, but she didn't want to say.

"What's happening to him?"

"He drank from the stream that she enchanted. There's a spell on it, or rather a kind of poison in it. He's becoming an animal."

"What animal?"

The woman rolled her lower lip in, bit it a little, then let it roll out again. "*Odocoileus virginianus ochrourus,* I think. It's a kind of deer. She hasn't used that one in a while." She stared at Sol, but her mind seemed to be elsewhere. "I think I can heal him, though. I've been working on it for a while, the cure. We'll see. And, as long as he hasn't had the last ingredients, I don't think the transformation will complete itself."

She breathed out a deep sigh, as if preparing herself. She squeezed her hands into fists, then opened them again. On one side of the cabin were woven baskets, and she went to these now. They were piled up on one another, some inside of others or half tilted atop. Filling each were leaves, or bark, or berries, or seeds, acorns, nuts, or roots. She took up a bowl, very wide and low-lipped. It was glazed and painted a repeating, leafy pattern.

She started filling the bowl with handfuls from different baskets. As she did, she talked quietly as if trying to remind herself of what to take. Every so often she frowned, looked at the bowl, and counted, checking what she had already.

Finally she put the bowl down on the floorboards and stepped over to a little triangular wood stand with three shelves. She took up several small jars, each painted a different colorful pattern. They were stoppered with old wood shards.

She opened each of the jars and smelled them. She poured some of their contents into a cup—a kind of dented metal camping cup.

"This first," she said. "It's the most important." She frowned at the cup for a moment, as if unsure, and smelled its aroma. "This is going to work," she said more to herself than to Connie, although she looked up and caught Connie's eye as she did. "It's going to. And then later, compresses and the tea." She nodded at the bowl of leaves and bark. "She's not going to win this time. You can help." She went to the cot. "Hold your brother up. Can you? He's your brother, right?"

"Yes," Connie said.

She helped hold Sol up while the woman put the cup to his lips. The liquid was thick and dark.

"It's not dangerous, is it?" Connie asked.

"Dangerous? I don't think so. It's just a question of working. What you should be worried about is his turning into an animal. Once he's a deer, he's finished. You understand that?"

"The animals in the stone house?"

"Yes, the hunter," she said. "There's a cursed hunter in these woods. The witch will wake him once your brother is a deer, and he'll hunt your brother down. Your brother will have no more sense than a deer. Understand? He'll be game, and inexperienced game at that." She tilted the cup as Connie held Sol's head. The woman said gently to Sol, "Come on, I know it tastes bad, but please, drink some. It'll help."

Sol took a sip, opening his eyes a crack.

"A little more." The woman poured in another sip and Sol swallowed again. "Okay, you can let him down now."

She put the cup on the floor and went to the bowl. She pulled out certain wide leaves. "These need to be wetted and placed against his armpits and on his forehead. Use the hot water from the stove. Put some in one of my bowls, steep the leaves in the water, then apply them. Do it carefully but as quickly as you can."

Connie started on this as the woman pulled two

wood coals out of the stove using tongs. She placed these very near the bottom of Sol's bare feet.

Following the Camper Lady's instructions, Connie put the leaves on Sol's armpits and head, over the hard bumps that Connie knew now were horns—or antlers, she thought, correcting herself like Sol would have. She went to look at his feet and felt that, because of the glowing coals below them, their bottoms were very hot. They were also smooth, the skin hardening. Into hooves, Connie thought.

"We've done what we can. The important things." The woman sat by the stove on a cushion that she pulled from a stack by the door. Her green cap was off now, but her hair, pressed against her head, was still in the shape of the cap.

"These"—she gestured to the herbs left in the bowl—"are for tea. But let him rest. We need to see if we've broken the fever."

She pushed a cushion over for Connie, who sat.

"The rain should keep her off, at least. Maybe she doesn't even know you're here yet, in my cabin."

"The witch?" Connie asked.

The woman didn't say anything for a long time, staring at the coals in the stove.

"The witch," she said finally. "Monique."

"And who are you?"

"I'm the one who's going to drive her from this valley. She's been here a very long time with no one to challenge her. Not anymore. Well, but I'm not able to challenge her directly yet. I'm new here, see? I'm not like the others. I'm only as old as I look. How old do I look?"

"Thirty?"

The woman almost laughed. "Always guess low." She glanced at Connie. "I'm sorry, I forgot. You must be starving. And thirsty. You don't have any water, do you? Not if your brother drank from the stream. Why didn't you, too?"

"He said one of us had to test it, to make sure it was safe."

The woman raised her eyebrows. "Really? That's some brother you've got there."

"Yeah," Connie agreed, nodding several times. "I drank a little of your hot water already, when I was making the leaves wet."

"Good. I've been so worried about your brother—I think I heard you call him Sol?—I forgot about you."

"It's okay. Sol's so sick. I'm just hungry."

The woman reached behind the woodstove and

took out several sacks. From one she pulled white knobby things, long, with green stems growing from one end. She handed them to Connie.

"Just what they look like, wild carrots. Washed already. Are you a big carrot eater?"

"Not really."

"They'll stave off the hunger. And they're good for you. But—you look like you need something more substantial. I've got just the thing, a special meal I made this week for myself." She took a pot near the wall, lifting it as if it was heavy, and set it beside the hot-water pot on the stove. "Just needs heating up."

She took off the cover and stirred it with a wooden spoon. The smell came at once to Connie, a very delicious one, some kind of soup.

"Be patient. It won't be good cold," the Camper Lady said. "Those carrots are good for you. Eat them first."

Connie chewed on the whitish carrots, which were crunchy and also a bit more bitter than normal carrots, less tasty, and Connie didn't like carrots to begin with. But she found she was so hungry, she ate all four.

The rain was starting to end, the drops less loud now on the roof, a soft patter.

Connie stood and walked over to Sol, who lay on the cot with his eyes closed. She leaned close to him. He had two short antlers over his eyes. His feet too, she saw when she looked there, were completely hardened, and the toes were hidden under smooth skin ending in an edge.

But his face looked more peaceful. He was finally sleeping, breathing normally. There was no longer a look of strain.

Connie stepped over to the cabin door, unlatched and opened it, staring out at the rain and the water that streamed off the cabin roof.

"Close that!" the woman said.

Connie did. The woman, apparently realizing her tone of voice, said, "I know I said she won't be out there now, with the rain. But you never can be too careful."

Connie nodded. "Sorry."

The woman twitched her head a little to the side. "Here, come and eat your supper." She stirred it and took up a bowl that looked hand-carved. She ladled the food into the bowl, a very thick soup with chunks in it.

"Stew," she said.

Connie took it and a spoon that the woman handed her. The food smelled terrific. Still, she hesitated.

"Rabbit," said the woman. "I have to live out here too. I don't just live on vegetables and nuts. Don't worry—it's a real rabbit. I can tell."

So Connie found herself, even with Sol turning into a deer that would be hunted, sitting down to a yummy meal of stew, and the meat was very tasty and gave her strength.

CHAPTER

14

HALF DEER

SOL WOKE STARING at a cabin ceiling. He felt much better. His headache was gone. His stomach felt almost normal. He turned his head and saw Connie sitting on a cushion, eating from a bowl on her lap. She hadn't noticed that he was awake yet. Next to her sat a woman in camping clothes. He recognized her, not so much from her appearance but because he had a mixed-up memory of everything that had happened while he lay ill. Except that, in his high fever, the woman's voice had sometimes been the voice of the All Creatures lady from Grand Creek, sometimes the voice of Holaderry the witch, sometimes the voice of his stepmother, Mrs. Blink, and sometimes even the voice of his old teacher Ms. Alma, besides being the woman's own voice.

Connie's voice, on the other hand, had always been Connie, even through his fever.

He sat up, and immediately the two heads turned to look at him. In Connie's face he saw both how helpless she was feeling with him being so sick and how happy—or relieved—she was to see him awake.

The woman's face, meanwhile, showed concern, curiosity, and something like shrewdness.

"Sol, you're up!"

Sol winced at Connie's loud cry as if he still had a terrible headache. He was so pleased when he realized it didn't hurt to hear even such a high-pitched cry. He smiled and, when she came over and put her hand on his shoulder, he put his hand on hers.

"I'm feeling much better," he said. "You can't imagine how I felt before. It was terrible."

"Is your fever really gone, Sol?"

"Gone. Fever, headache. Connie, that was a terrible headache. Feeling nauseous. I feel . . . fine."

Sol felt a little foolish saying this, since his chest was covered in long hair—fur. His feet, sticking out below his pants, looked like hooves. His legs, what he could see of them, were as thin as bone and thickly furred. They also felt sore, like after a long exercise, but strong. And longer than usual. He put his hand to his forehead and felt antlers. Smooth. When he touched them, he felt the touch as pressure where they met his head. Putting his hands to the back of his neck, he found that his long hair had turned into something like a mane. It was more tangled than his hair had been.

He was very warm too, despite his fever being gone. That was because of his fur, he thought, and the heat of the woodstove. But Sol didn't feel awful like before. He felt, if anything, full of energy. The woman, who came up next to Connie, gave him a curious look, as if wondering what was going on in Sol's head. She put her hand on his shoulder like Connie had, a touch Sol felt as strange. It made him nervous.

"You've been treating me. Thank you," Sol said to her.

She took her hand off, as if sensing how he felt. "There's still more to do, though," she said. "A lot more."

"I can see that. But—I'm feeling so much better."

As if to prove it, he stood. It was strange to stand on his new legs. They were powerful. And he found he was as tall as an adult. His eyes were even with the woman's eyes, and he was looking more than usual down at Connie. And that was with his legs slightly bent, a position that felt right to Sol.

Connie had stepped back as he rose.

He walked across the cabin. He bobbed a little up and down as he did. His hooves clicked against the floorboards.

"I'm fast," he said to Connie. He ran across the cabin. It was only a few steps to him, so he didn't get a chance to reach any speed.

He'd get to do that later.

The woman smiled at Sol's spurt of energy, then frowned. "Now, sit down. The cabin can't handle someone in your condition. We've still got a ways to go."

"Sorry," Sol said, taking a couple more strong steps, *click-click*ing his hooves, which he felt were so strong and hard that he could have kicked someone with them and it would have hurt.

Like the witch.

He put his head down a little and peered at Connie as if about to charge. Their eyes met. Sol pulled up.

"It's okay," Sol said to her. "I feel okay."

He sat on a cushion on the floor. He felt funny at how far he had to bend to sit down. His arms were much longer too when he put his hands to the floor to lower himself the last bit onto the cushion. He glanced at the woman. He had a vague memory of her with a green cap, but she'd taken it off now. She was ladling water out of the larger of two pots, filling a cup that she handed to Sol. The cup had scenes of the four seasons painted on it.

"Drink that," she said. "You've got to drink the whole pot's worth."

"I'm getting better, right?"

The woman didn't answer as surely as he would have liked. "I think you are. You're on the path to recovery."

"I *feel* better." Sol didn't want to admit it, but if someone had told him right then that he could be turned back to the boy he'd been, he almost wouldn't have wanted it. He glanced at Connie. Could she tell?

"You've changed so much, Sol," Connie said, as if reading his thoughts.

"I know, Connie. But it doesn't feel bad anymore, see? That headache, it was like I couldn't feel anything else, just the awful pain. That's stopped. And look on the bright side." He smiled. "I could outrun anything now. And my fur will keep me warm."

"It's not funny," Connie said.

"I know it isn't, Connie. I just—I don't want you to worry. At least I'm feeling well enough to joke. We're going to make it, don't you see, Connie? The witch, she made a mistake. I heard that in my fever, right? I didn't imagine it?" he asked the woman.

"No. She dropped one bag of ingredients on her

way to the mountain spring that feeds the streams by the road. She must have been in a rush."

The woman found the small bag where she'd left it by the stove, and held it up.

"Can I see?" Sol asked.

He took it and opened it. He smelled. He realized that he had a very developed sense of smell now. He could smell each of the ingredients in the bag separately, even though they mixed into a single scent. One aroma was sweet, another bitter like bark, and a third was something else, rotten or putrid.

There was something familiar about the scents too. Almost as if he'd tasted them already, after all.

"Be careful," Connie said.

"I'm not eating it, Connie."

"But it's natural for us to worry about you," the woman said. "I'm glad you're feeling so much better. My concoction seems to be working. And without those last ingredients, you might never turn completely into an animal. But the thing is, I have to admit—I lost the last child. He turned completely."

That didn't sound comforting to Sol.

"But he drank the whole potion, with all of the ingredients?" Sol asked. "From the stream?"

She nodded.

Sol thought about that. "He became an elk?"

"Yes." The woman sounded surprised. "How did you know?"

"We saw him," Sol said.

"Where?"

"When we first walked in," Connie said.

"Well, it is true that he had a sort of luck after all," the woman admitted. "He'll never be a boy again, but he was one of the very few to last a whole season against David, the hunter. It's an old hunting rule. Any animal that's hunted for a season and survives is never hunted again. That animal has earned the right to live the rest of its natural life here in the valley, even if the hunter finds it later. And Theo made it. Theodore was his name. He was very careful as an elk. It was almost like he was born to be an elk, that Monique did him a favor by turning him. Still, *I* failed." She paused. "I still have something of his."

She reached behind the baskets along the wall and pulled out a little pad. She flipped through it in front of them. It had pages of slanted kid writing, words ending at the very edge, and some of them missing letters because there wasn't space. There were drawings too, of dragons and monsters and rounded figures with long swords. She put it down beside her.

"But," she said, "what you saw might have been a real elk."

"No," Sol answered, very sure. "It was him. I can feel it, especially now. I think we found his knife too. Is there no way to turn *him* back?"

"That depends," the woman answered. "If you can believe the old story, it's said that long ago an older sister and younger brother came into these woods, crossed the valley, and escaped. The brother was only five or so, and he drank from the stream and turned into a deer. But the sister, who had powers like me and Monique and others, she heard the stream whispering to her and so didn't drink. The two managed to escape the valley with the help of hunters. *The* hunter, David. He carried the girl and her brother to the edge of the valley. The one and only time he ever helped children. I don't think anyone knows what happened to them later, whether the sister was able to turn her brother back to a human or not.

"But it's said they left something behind, something

that can reverse the witch's magic. I can't tell you if that's true or not—the sister or the brother must have been very powerful to do such a thing. But it *is* possible. Still," she went on, "Theo has been an elk for three winters. I don't think whatever they left behind would work for him. There's not much boy left in him by now, if there ever was much boy in Theo to start with. And the place is hidden. Nobody knows what was left behind or how to use it. Not the witch. Not me. Monique has searched long in this valley and never found it. I think it must be past the mountain peaks where Monique can't go, outside the valley, that they left it behind after they crossed over the mountain pass. There's no way to reach it or find it, then, so we'll have to wait—to see about you." She nodded toward the cup in Sol's hands. "Drink," she said.

Sol took a sip. It tasted something like hot water full of grass. Normally he would have gagged, but he found there was something pleasing in the flavor. The bitterness of the grass tasted just right, as if his body needed what was in the tea and had been missing it.

The woman, when he looked, appeared to be watching his reaction carefully.

He smiled and said, "It's not bad, really."

He took another sip.

She looked satisfied. "Good. I'm glad. I won't feed you any rabbit stew. I don't think you'd like it. Or that it would be good for you."

Sol knew what she was talking about, and he agreed. He could smell the stew from Connie's bowl, even though it wasn't that near. He didn't like the smell of meat in it. It didn't smell like something you could eat at all. It wasn't that the meat was spoiled, exactly, but it smelled that way to him. Deer don't eat meat, Sol realized.

What else has changed about me? he wondered.

His hearing was better. Sol heard the raindrops on the roof, extremely loud. When he listened, he could hear exactly where each drop struck. The rain was letting up.

Sol's fingers also felt very stiff. It hurt to bend them.

The woman, meanwhile, was telling more about the witch and the hunter. "For centuries, Monique turned children who came into these woods into animals," she explained. "Hunters galloped in on horseback, unaware, or so they claimed, that some of the animals were children. Monique herself always said that she wasn't doing anything too bad. That it was the hunters who should have known better. And it's true the hunters *had* heard rumors of a witch in these woods and children disappearing. This valley was even called the accursed valley in those days. But they hunted anyway once they discovered they could ride in and out, and how full the woods were of game."

"Of what?" asked Connie.

"Game is what hunters call the animals they hunt," Sol explained.

The woman nodded. She went on, "But Monique could only play tricks on the hunters for so long. The best of them, David Bittworth, who'd hunted more children-turned-into-animals than anyone else, David finally had second thoughts when he came face-to-face with that sister who hadn't turned into an animal but whose brother had. The ones I told you about. He wounded the brother first in the leg. But then he helped the two children, and that's how they escaped." She described the hunter's ride for Sol and Connie, how the rest of the hunting party was frozen still by Monique on their horses, and how David couldn't escape, since he'd participated for too long hunting in the valley. He could only drop the children off.

"Monique knew no more hunters would ride into this valley after that hunting party never returned. Certainly not if anyone ever rode in and saw the hunters on their horses, frozen still. But it didn't matter by then, because she'd caught David. The best of them all. She completed the curse on him—that curse is simply that he must keep doing, eternally, what he already did. *He must keep enjoying himself,* is how Monique would put it, I think. David falls into a long sleep whenever children are coming, then Monique wakes him, always in the morning once the children are turned. She has given him enchanted arrows to hunt with so that the animals grow totally still. Preserved. David brings them back after, to the stone lodge where he lives, and Monique poses them in the central room. They can be placed in any pose, and they'll stay that way. Monique wants David to live with his prey." The woman pursed her lips. "It's why we have to keep you from changing all the way, Sol, and you from turning at all, Connie. As long as you two haven't changed, you still have a chance. Monique won't wake David until then. But once one of you

143

turns, you're *fair game*, as the expression goes. David will hunt you, and he'll succeed too. He's the best at what he does."

She stopped talking, rose, and stepped to the door, opening it a crack and looking out.

"It's quiet," she said. "Too quiet. I don't like it."

She closed the door again and latched it shut.

"But I didn't drink from the stream," Connie said. "So I won't change."

"Oh, she'll find a way to turn you too."

"And I haven't changed all the way," Sol said.

He fell silent for a while, thinking.

"What does she look like?" he asked. "Monique."

"She's very hard to see," the Camper Lady said. "Much of the time she's just a shadow, a darkness that can grow very large. You can only see her if she wants you to. If you *do* see her, though—" She paused. "She's very old. Old as the mountains and as crooked as a tree branch."

As she spoke those words, Sol could almost see Monique in his mind's eye, what she looked like. Crooked and old.

That bent old witch stared at Sol in his mind.

Got you, she said to him.

Sol shook his head.

"Lucky you found us," he said.

"Yes, isn't it?" She smiled. She reached over to Connie's bowl. "All finished?"

Connie nodded. The bowl was empty. She had had two bowls' worth, actually. It was a very yummy rabbit stew. It made her a little sleepy after not eating anything all day. She looked over at Sol and started to worry again, which woke her up. He said he felt better, and obviously he did. But it didn't look like he was turning back into a boy.

She glanced then at the woman, who was also looking at Sol. The woman turned to meet Connie's gaze and made a face like she understood what Connie was thinking, and that she was worried too.

Meanwhile, Sol was saying, "Well, we're going to defeat this witch, this Monique. Just like we did to Holaderry."

The woman seemed startled by this remark.

"What did you say?" she asked.

"Holaderry, the witch in Grand Creek. We beat *her*. How do you think we made it this far?"

"I thought that you were runaways. They come up

from Grand Creek, if they discover soon enough what their parents are up to. Giving them to the witch for her meals." She hesitated. "Are you saying Fay Holaderry is gone?"

"Yep, I pushed her into the fire pit myself." Sol sounded proud, which he was. "We—we didn't think there were more. We thought we were on our way to safety. Our aunt's." He stood, feeling very tall again, his hooves clicking against the floorboards. He went to his knapsack and brought it over. "Look, we've even got her journal." He took Holaderry's journal out. "Stole it from her house. We're going to read it all, someday." He opened it, paging through. He remembered something. "Just before I went to sleep last night, I tried to read in the journal. I thought it might have something about the woods here. But I've been sick all day."

The woman said, "Fay Holaderry has been keeping a journal? Do you really think she included the secrets of these woods in there too? I don't think that would be allowed by the others."

"The others who?" Connie asked.

"Other witches and evil creatures."

"You really know a lot about them."

"Enough," she said to Connie.

"Here," Sol said, stopping on a page. *"Other Witches, Less Famous but Just as Wicked as Me."*

Sol read aloud:

Children everywhere are in danger. From what? you might ask. Or maybe you should ask, From whom? From ogres, ghosts, goblins, trolls (who don't always live in caves or forests anymore, but often in houses), and of course from people like me and my brethren.

They call us witches, *brujas, penyihir, majo, sorcières.* Everywhere in the world they tell children stories about us—old, traditional stories. But, unfortunately for the children, adults recount the stories as if they took place far away and long ago. They don't want to frighten the kids too much, they say. And so children aren't prepared.

I am possibly the most famous of us all, since I cook and eat children.

But for sheer evilness, no one can outdo a witch named Daisy who turns children into firewood and puts them into her fireplace.

"They are very kind to make sure that an old woman like me doesn't freeze," she told me once. "Those sweet little darlings warm my heart . . . and my toes."

And then there is the witch of the woods, the queen of the accursed valley, Monique.

Sol looked up when he got to that name. Both Connie and the woman were staring at him intently. He went on:

She lives just near me, a neighbor, you might say. She specializes in children on the run. Children who are all alone in the world and have no one to watch out for them. She turns them to animals, and then she wakes a hunter, a cursed man who, because he once hunted such animals, now must always do so.

Monique loves turning into a shadow so that you can't see her, she loves her enchantments and the trickery by which she turns the kids into beasts, and she loves very much sending her hunter forth to hunt the children down. She collects them, like a girl with her stuffed animals, and keeps them in the lodge where the hunter lives. . . .

Sol's voice suddenly trailed off. He was clearly reading on. He even turned the page. But then he shut the book and looked up, first at the woman and then at Connie. To Connie he looked frightened, but something in his expression also made her not ask what was wrong.

"She just goes on about that awful hunter and the stone lodge," Sol said. "Where we were. I looked inside, and I can't get those animals out of my head. The children, some of them were staring out the window straight at me. I don't want to read any more about them." Sol swallowed. "But we'll beat this Monique, I know it. With your help, of course. You've been"—his voice trailed off again—"very helpful," he said in a hoarse whisper, then cleared his throat.

He put the journal back into his knapsack. All the time, Sol's mind was racing, trying to think how they might get out of the cabin.

Because what he'd actually read was this:

She wanders the woods, looking for all the world like a forest ranger with that green cap of hers and the way she's kept her youthful look. She convinces children that she'll help them against the terrible witch. Ha!

Then Monique brings them back to her log cabin and does with them what she will.

CHAPTER

15

FLIGHT

THE THRUSH WAS IN FRONT of the witch's cabin. In the morning, it had finally reached the first mountain peak, flown past a hawk's nest, and darted down the mountainside into the woods of the accursed valley. It had searched everywhere near the road and even around the stone lodge. Finally it had headed for the cabin.

The thrush was too late. It was able to hear voices inside, not just the voice of the witch but the voices of children. *The* children, it must have been.

They were in there.

The manager had told the thrush not to be seen. But this was an emergency. What should it do?

❧

SOL stepped to the door, unlatched it, saying, "It sure is hot in here," and opened it.

The Camper Lady—Monique—went right over, stepped gently in front of Sol, and closed the door calmly.

"I don't want anyone to see you two here," she said. "The witch has spies in these woods. I think I saw a small bird outside just now, for instance, that was acting a bit strange. If it saw you, it might carry the news back to the witch. We have to keep her from knowing for as long as possible. Don't we?"

She smiled.

As she spoke, Sol once again saw an old witch in his mind, out there in the woods. A terrible, crooked old woman, not this kind one here. No, he thought. This woman says anything, and you start to believe her.

"Please, it's so . . . hot in here," Sol said. "Maybe we can open a window."

"Of course, if it makes you feel better."

As she turned to push the window shutter open, Sol was frantically pointing to Connie's pack and the door.

Connie knew something was up, of course—she knew Sol so well. Something to do with why he'd stopped reading. She nodded.

Just then, as Monique turned away from the window, a wood thrush landed on the sill, singing loudly.

Connie ran for her knapsack. And Sol, in an unexpected move, turned with his back to the witch, jumped onto his hands, and kicked his hind legs at her with all his might.

"Run!" he shouted. "Connie, run!"

Connie ran for the door and fiddled with the latch. She got it open. Sol's hoof struck a blow to Monique in the center of her chest. She fell with a crash backward into her baskets of leaves. Standing on his hooves again, Sol grabbed his knapsack and ran through the doorway, picking Connie up when he reached her. His arms were so strong that he did so with little effort. Connie was surprised but held on to his shoulders tight as he sped between the trees on his deer legs. His hooves came down, just missing the roots. The thrush appeared flying in front of Sol. Sol was unsure what it wanted. He thought of the bird as the witch's spy, just as Monique had said it was. But then he changed his mind. *She* had given him that idea, he realized. And if the witch said the thrush was a spy, maybe it was—but against her, not for her.

Meanwhile, Monique was calling from her doorway. "That's it, run! Run fast. It's good for you to try out your new legs, Sol. Let your sister down! Hop along after your brother, Connie! I'll go wake David!"

Sol leaped over dead logs, holding Connie up. The thrush was trying to get Sol to run in a different direction. He turned, following it, hoping it knew something he didn't. They came into the open by the river. Sol felt an instinctive fear. He was an easy target in such a place. He didn't know when he'd become afraid of being hunted, but he was. Sol ran down to the water, dodging left and right, following the little bird, which flew right over the river, seeming not to notice for a while that Sol and Connie had stopped.

"Whose bird is it, do you think?" Sol asked Connie as he put her down quickly.

"I don't know. Maybe the woman in the pet store? With the cane? She had birds like that."

"Where is it leading us?"

"Out of these woods, Sol. I want to get out."

Sol scratched low on his neck with his hand, which had no fingers. They had grown together, or rather a tough skin had grown over them. He had to fight the urge to lean forward onto his arms.

"No," he said. "I don't think so. At least . . . Connie, if I make it out of this forest, I'll still be a deer."

"Maybe it's leading us to that place," Connie said.

"The one no one knows?" Sol asked.

The bird came back, landed in front of them, then took off and fluttered over the river again, landing on the other side. It was a long stone's throw across, the distance from center field to home plate. It was easy to see the other side.

The bird called from there.

"We can't get across so easily," Sol called out, wondering if it could understand him. "Is there a crossing?"

The bird tweeted and called and sang. Maybe it was trying to tell them something, but Sol didn't know what. It flew across to them, flew over to the other side again, then cried out.

"I guess it doesn't know another way across," Sol said. "A bird just doesn't think about these things. They don't need bridges."

This was no slow-moving river that they might

have swum across normally. Its currents swept by fast—not as rapids, but fast enough.

"Connie, look, we're both good swimmers. And I'm strong now, stronger than usual. You hold on to me, and I'll swim us across. I think we can make it. We might end up downstream some, but I think we can make it. What do you think?"

"I think so, Sol. We can do it."

"Wear your backpack so it won't come off." Sol already had his on his back. Connie had been holding hers in front.

With that, he picked up Connie, who clutched his neck, which was thick and powerful now and covered in fur. Sol splashed in. The water was very cold. It soaked his pants. He felt the current pulling on his legs. As soon as it was deep enough to sweep him off his feet, he went in forward and began, naturally, to paddle with his legs and arms, an animal's paddle.

I can make it, he thought. But the current was fierce. It swept him and Connie downriver. It was all he could do to keep his head up. The water splashed into his face, and he swallowed. Connie was hanging on. He could feel her arms digging into his neck and her hands clasped under his Adam's apple. That was choking him too.

Connie's head, meanwhile, was underwater. She pulled up and gasped. Then her head went underwater again. She felt her fingers being pulled apart as she tried to hold on to Sol. Her hands slipped a little, then more, and suddenly she lost her grip completely. And just like that, Connie was swept away downriver.

CHAPTER

IN THE CURRENTS

WATER SWEPT OVER CONNIE. Of all the frightening moments in all their adventures, this was the most frightening. She was carried like a leaf caught on the front of a bicycle. The river filled her ears; everything was a gurgle. Her eyes were closed. She was in darkness. Her lungs hurt as she held her breath. She couldn't breathe. Finally she was able to twist herself and shoot up. She broke the surface, took a breath, saw the sky and a flash of trees by the bank, then was pulled under again.

Her knapsack and clothes were pulling her down. She pushed her arms back and let the knapsack slip away. She cared nothing about the things she was losing. She just wanted to reach the surface. She had no time to take off her jumper. The current was pushing her legs over her and her head down. She was sinking deeper, away from air and light above. She needed a breath right away. She opened her arms wide and stopped holding her legs together. She somersaulted underwater. The current pushed her up then, and she broke the surface again. She blew out in the open air and breathed in as water splashed across her face. With her arms held out, she was able to stay floating at the top of the river. She saw rocks sticking up ahead. For a moment she steered to try to climb onto them. But she was going so fast. She realized that she would be thrown hard against the rocks—some underwater too. It was dangerous. Instead she let the current take her past the boulders and into the middle of the river. But there she was being pulled downstream incredibly fast toward rippling white water.

Swim at an angle to the current, Sol had taught her one day when they'd visited a beach. Connie tried it, swimming in a direction not exactly with the current but not too much against it either. Her flailing arms and wild kicks seemed like nothing as she was pushed at a tremendous speed, the woods going by on both sides. Her strokes had almost no effect—but almost no effect was different from none at all. She *was* a good swimmer. She was pulling out to the side.

Before she knew it, she was near the riverbank in a slow part of the river. She grabbed at plants that grew in the water. Finally she felt her shoes scrape the river bottom. She made it farther toward the bank, onto her knees. Rocks cut into her shins. She was hurt. She slid in the current.

She stood, walked out, and fell onto the bank, coughing and unable to stop. Her body seized with each cough. She spun around to lie on her back, but that choked her too much. She sat up and leaned between her knees until she could finally breathe. She took deep breaths, as slowly as she could. They rasped in her wet throat. A few more coughs, and she felt, leaning over, head almost on the ground, that she was okay. She glanced up. She was on the side of the river they had started from, she thought. Across, on the other side, the land rose in a cliff.

She wrapped her arms around herself. She felt chilled. Her jumper, all wet, stuck to her. She stood and walked away from the river. She sat between the trees, which were extremely big here—gigantic.

⁓⁂⁓

"CONNIE!"

As Connie was swept away from him, Sol screamed from the river so loudly, louder than he'd ever screamed in his life. Water splashed and filled his mouth. He choked. He leaned his head back. He coughed, took a breath, and put his head underwater. He paddled and paddled.

His feet—his hooves—hit bottom. A little farther, and he stood tall. He struggled hard to get out of the current, fell sideways, was swept down a bit farther, gained his footing again, and pushed himself shallower. He strode out onto the bank and collapsed.

Alone.

That's not true—the thrush was there too.

"Find her!" he shouted at it.

The thrush flew off at a height just a few feet above the water. Soon it disappeared around a curve downriver. Sol dragged himself out of sight from the other riverbank—and the witch—through tangled leafy brush that was wet from the rain. Sol himself was soaking wet and cold. But that was soon to be the least of his problems. He closed his eyes to protect them from branches, until he discovered that his antlers pushed the branches away.

He reached a clear spot—a few feet of grass between spindly plants that surrounded him like a cage or a bird-watching blind.

The witch Monique, he realized, had fed him the last ingredients in her cabin. That black drink and the tea. Pretending to heal him. He had never been getting better.

He was changing all the way now.

At first it was almost laughable. Thick brown fur grew from every pore on his skin, tingling like mad. Except it grew gray-white on his chest. With his hardening hands, he felt his furry face.

But his muscles ached too. He leaned forward, his antlers near the ground, feeling the pain. Cracking sounds came from his neck. That scared Sol. It sounded as if his neck were breaking. But he felt better with each crack. His neck felt like it was finally stretching out after years of being trapped.

A sudden severe pain in his back made him snap his head up, his lips curling over long teeth. The pain grew worse—Sol's world was nothing but pain then. Thankfully, it passed, and he collapsed forward onto his arms. He breathed deeply, over and over again, until he realized that he was panting, his tongue hanging out of his mouth.

A cracking—like the one in his neck—started in his arms now. He felt it as if inside his arms there were a chain tugging forward on his bones. The pain was agonizing. He clenched his teeth to bear it and squeezed his eyes shut. He heard himself whimpering. His furry arms were growing. Not quite fast enough to see. But painful minutes later, they were long like legs and bone-thin. At their ends, far away, his hands were gone, just curved hooves.

Suddenly Sol worried not that he was turning, but that it wouldn't work right. Did kids always grow into animals well, or did some kids grow wrong, with ribs popping out of their chests or antlers growing from their knees?

Was this late stage in the change supposed to be so hard?

Sol spent what seemed like forever—would it never end?—writhing in his hiding place, stretching, twisting, and rolling onto his back, until he finally got another breather. The pain lessened to an ache.

He lay still.

He saw the thrush returning to the riverbank.

"Here!" he called to it. The word stuck in his throat. His voice was low and not very clear.

But the thrush heard him and flew over. It landed

on the ground and sang a short, sad melody. Sol thought, rightly, that it hadn't found Connie.

"She'll make it out," Sol croaked, his voice rough as if very hoarse. "I know she will. She can't drown. The river could have swept her farther down. We have to go farther."

He struggled to stand on all fours, his head, still human but furry, sticking out forward on a deer's neck. Most of his aches and pains were gone now, or maybe it was just that fear for Connie filled him with new strength.

Sol broke through his cover into the open by the river, and he started to run. His clothes had torn and split. Now they fell off him completely, though his knapsack stayed on his deer's back. He found himself springing off his back legs and landing on his front legs, which he pushed forward as his back legs hit the ground for another leap. Like that, he sprang fast through the woods. He heard his breath as he did, a repeated *huh-huh-huh-huh-huh*.

But he couldn't keep up such a pace for long. He fell into a run where one front leg and the opposite back leg moved together. This was still very fast. With each step, he felt as if he was pushing forward the whole length of his body. He crashed through the brush and bushes. His long antlers pushed branches out of his way before they came near his eyes. He got close to the riverbank and kept an eye out for Connie. For a while, the land he was on rose steeply. He ended up high over the water. The bank had risen into a cliff, and he was on its top. The river ran fast below, its rush echoing up the cliff face.

Sol's ears twisted one way and the other as he listened. He moved forward to stand at the edge of the cliff, his back legs far behind and his front legs just by the drop. That way he could look down, stretching his neck forward. When he did, he saw that the currents were white and splashed around boulders.

There was nowhere on Sol's side that Connie could wash up onto. The cliff fell straight into the river. On the other side, though, was woods. If she'd gotten out there, he might not see her. He peered across. She could have gone into the woods.

He ran on. The cliff sloped down—or the river rose—and soon he was running alongside the water again between trees. Speeding up, he went on for as long as he could, always watching the other side, but the pain he'd been ignoring—all through his limbs—became too strong for him.

Don't give up, he thought.

He found a hidden place instinctively. Many wild animals will hide if they are sick. This was a wide slope covered in what looked like ferns. He lay on his side, his long legs pointing outward, so that he was under a roof of fern leaves a foot above him. He breathed deeply with his mouth open. He felt how his cheek against the ground was very long. His head was the wrong shape. He heard his bones cracking. With each crack came relief.

MONIQUE'S FAVORITE PLACE

MONIQUE STRAIGHTENED UP the cabin. She'd fallen into her stacked baskets when Sol had kicked her. Herbs lay scattered across the floor, all mixed together now. Splinters of bark had slid into curly brown leaves. Dried-out flower petals stuck to the outside of nuts. She swept it carefully to the side. It would take hours to sort through it all, separate the ingredients, and put them into their proper baskets. She'd do it when this was all over, which wouldn't be long now.

She stacked the baskets back into place, half empty, putting her hand to the center of her chest as she did, feeling the bruise there. She unbuttoned her camping shirt to look: the bruise was a dark blue mark, the shape of a hoof. It was always a little dangerous to have wild animals inside the cabin, she thought, smiling to herself.

Sol's shirt, pants, socks, and sneakers lay in the corner where Connie had put them after changing Sol into fresh clothes. Monique picked up the socks and stuffed them into one of her shirt pockets. She put the bowl Connie had been eating from into a wooden bucket that she used to bring dirty dishes down to the river. But she pocketed the spoon Connie had been eating with, after wiping it clean. She shuttered the windows, latching them so that animals couldn't get into the cabin while she was gone. She twisted her ponytail, tied it back, and put on her green cap.

Stepping outside, she shut the door to the cabin firmly. The air smelled of rain, though the rain had stopped. To anyone else, this forest would have looked like a wilderness. But to her, it was home. She struck out on a narrow trail that few would have noticed. She crossed the brook that she and Connie had come across with Sol on her shoulder. Then the land sloped to a high, wide rock that she could either climb or bushwhack around. On a day like today, it would be wet and muddy going around, so she climbed up it. Once on top, she had to work her way down the slippery slant of rock on the other side. Then there was a nice curving trail through the forest. She heard a woodpecker's *tap-tap-tap* and looked up but couldn't see it through the leafy branches.

The climb to the lodge grew steep. Many people would have been winded by the path. Kids from towns and cities always had trouble with such steep slopes. Monique herself was in excellent condition.

As she hiked, she thought about Sol and Connie. They were very clever, those two, but still they had fallen for her act. Tell the kids there's something terrible *out there*, and they stick to you like glue.

And they'd really had a chance to escape the valley too, because she *had* dropped that bag of ingredients in her rush to the spring. She'd discovered her mistake only later, counting the empty bags back at her cabin and finding that one was missing. She'd had to go all the way back to the spring, and there the bag had been, hanging from a branch. Too late to add its ingredients to the flowing water. So she'd had to lure Sol and Connie in to get Sol that final mixture. Plus, Connie hadn't drunk from the stream at all. Who knows how long she might have lasted because of Sol's careful measures, testing the water first?

Not anymore.

Monique had had so much fun today. Connie had

actually helped Monique pour the foul mixture down Sol's throat, and Connie had put the compresses on his armpits and forehead that helped bring out Sol's fur and antlers. Sol had drunk the tea Monique had made him. And Connie had eaten the stew and the wild carrots. Brilliant! Monique would think back often, she was sure, to the day Sol and Connie had visited her cabin, and she'd describe it more than once to her evil friends.

She reached the last stopping point before the lodge, half boulder and half grass. She had a view from there over much of the valley. It was a breathtaking sight, the treetops below, the river snaking along at the center of the valley. It was one advantage to being a witch of the woods. Monique had never wanted to live anywhere else. She couldn't understand witches who lived in towns.

She could see the spot where her cabin was in the woods below, although the cabin itself couldn't be seen. The trees hid it. She saw the place where Sol and Connie must have gone when they'd run from her cabin with the wood thrush. They'd headed north. Maybe they had managed to cross the river.

Monique walked on—it wasn't far now. The lodge

was hidden behind wild berry bushes. It was built against a rocky hill whose top could be reached only by hiking the sloping woodland around it. A tiny stream ran down that rock face, spreading out in places. Behind the tangle of bushes was the door. The old horn hung over it. Branches reached out in front, hung with berries. She pushed them aside and walked in.

The room she entered was her favorite place in all the valley, because it held her collection. She couldn't keep the collection in her cabin, of course, since she sometimes brought kids back there. The cabin was much too small, besides. And she liked it that David lived here—that he must see, every day, those he had hunted.

Still, it was *her* collection. The Animals of the Lodge, she called it. She invited her friends, other witches and evil creatures, to see it. No one else had such a room.

She posed the kids however she wished. She still thought of them as kids, although they had turned into animals. She knew all their names. She moved them often, placing one to catch the late afternoon light through the lodge window, another by the door

so that you saw him or her at once when you came in. She put a few small ones on the mantel over the fireplace and others near the fire pokers, posing them as if they were dancing, scratching, or leaping.

That's what was good about the way they froze under David's arrows, which she enchanted. It was better than stuffing them like in a regular museum. Every part of their bodies could still be moved, and they would stay that way, however they were positioned. She could rearrange them anytime she wished, dreaming up new poses. She thought that it was time for some rearranging now. Soon she'd pose Sol and Connie here, after all—forever stilled in her valley.

She had beaten them, of that she was sure.

Monique built a fire from kindling and logs stacked beside the fireplace, using the box of long matches that sat atop the mantelpiece to light it. It was late in the afternoon, and the rainy day had seeped into the lodge. She blew until the fire was strong, then sat in the chair before it. She could see a lot in the flickering flames.

For a time, her mind wandered to places only a centuries-old witch could know.

Evening fell. It grew dark outside the windows.

Finally she stood and walked quietly through the low stone doorway into the bedroom. That bedroom looked a little like a cave, since its ceiling was the inside of the stone hill itself. She sat on a stool by the bed. David lay there, sleeping peacefully. Mr. Sleepy-Head, she sometimes called him.

It was David's turn now. Monique loved sending him out on the hunt. He should have his fun too, she believed—and yes, it was fun for him, Monique was sure of that. Even if David never liked to admit it.

She pulled the blanket up to cover his broad shoulders.

"I'll wake you in the morning, David," she said softly. "And you will ride."

CHAPTER

18

RIDDLES THREE

CONNIE WAS IN A PART of the woods that might have been the oldest of all. The trees were gigantic, so big that she could walk around one trunk as if she were walking around the front yard and back yard of a house.

Afternoon had passed, and the woods were growing dark. Shadowy shapes around her looked like creatures, even monsters, although she knew that was all in her mind. She imagined one of the giant trees might open up and something would come out. There was enough room inside the trees for even a big monster to live quite comfortably.

She collected leaves and pine needles like she and Sol had done the night before. A lot of them fell out of her arms, so it took a long time. She made a pile of the leaves and needles in a dry spot. The woods were still wet from the rain, but here, where the giant trees were, there were many dry spots protected by leafy limbs like a roof very far overhead. She kept piling up leaves for as long as she could.

Sol, where are you? she wondered. She had called his name for a long time. But not as loudly as she could. She was worried about being found by others.

Like the witch.

Connie couldn't believe that the witch had tricked them. Connie had always thought she could look people in the eyes and tell what they were thinking, and especially if they were nice or not. But the Camper Lady had been convincing. She had seemed so truly concerned.

Now Connie lay on her pile, but it gave way. She found she was lying on the hard ground with leaves and pine needles sticking into her. She had often told herself she would like living in the great outdoors and camping. She loved nature and natural things. But, she realized, she still had a lot to learn. She and Sol had gone camping only once and not in a place like this.

Connie felt a bug crawling on her, and she

brushed it away. Right after that, she felt the illusion of other bugs on her skin in lots of places at once. She rubbed herself until the feeling went away.

She closed her eyes and tried to sleep.

She tossed and turned.

Eventually, exhaustion from everything that had happened overcame her, and she slept.

Almost at once, she had a dream.

SHE found herself walking into the All Creatures, Big and Small, shop in Grand Creek. A bell rang overhead as the door opened. Four dogs ran up to her, licking her hands and pushing their noses against her.

The All Creatures manager came out of the back room.

Connie had forgotten how big the manager was. The manager had a tiny blue flower pinned to her chest, which made her look all the bigger. She walked with the ancient duck-head cane clicking on the floor as she strode past aisles of pet products, some of which weren't pet products at all but objects from Connie's childhood—things from her room before they'd moved to Grand Creek, like a turtle-shaped pillow she'd always liked.

"Connie," the manager said, "you made it."

Connie always felt like the manager could read her thoughts just by looking at her. And so Connie was quieter than usual around the manager—a little shy, even.

"*Sitz*," the manager commanded the dogs, who stepped back and sat, staring at Connie.

A black cat strode out of the shadows of the shop. Quantum, thought Connie, but then she remembered it couldn't be. She had had to give Quantum away to a friend. Still, when she looked down, it *was* Quantum. She picked him up.

I miss you, she thought.

I miss you too, Quantum seemed to think back.

Connie stroked Quantum and looked up at the woman.

"Am I really here?" she asked.

"What do you think?"

No, Connie thought. I'm lying alone in the woods. She could even feel that her jumper was still a little wet. And there were leaves and pine needles stuck to her.

"We're in trouble," Connie said. "Big trouble. I almost"—Connie paused—"drowned. In the river.

I lost Sol, and he's turning into a deer, and a hunter is going to hunt him, and the witch here, Monique, she tricked us." Connie's voice rose. Telling it all, suddenly it was too much for her. "I don't know what to do. . . ."

She began to cry. Her tears streamed down her cheeks and fell on Quantum. One of the dogs, a black Labrador, broke from its place and trotted to her, licking her hand. The manager held her place, though, leaning on her cane and looking down at Connie.

Connie brushed away her tears and wiped her nose.

"Listen, we don't have long," the manager said quietly. "You must remember everything I tell you. You don't just have to escape the woods. You must reverse the spell. Lenore left a way." Sadness crept into her voice. She lifted her cane into the air. "Because you and Sol brought this back, *ohne Augen*, I can do this much, but no more. I have three riddles for you."

"Riddles?" Oh, no, Connie thought. "But I'm no good at riddles. Sol is. You should ask Sol."

The manager raised her large shoulders, then lowered them. "That's not possible anymore. Do you

understand?" She went on, "*You* must solve all three. And it's not like last time. There's no consolation prize." The manager fell silent. She seemed to be waiting for an answer.

Connie nodded. "Can you make them easy at least?" she asked.

A cloud passed over the manager's face.

"I'm doing everything I can." She sounded upset. "Everything, and I sent help too. This is it. Listen carefully. Here's the first one:

> *"I'm sometimes called what you are called—*
> *With you so much I share.*
> *But when you in a mirror stare,*
> *You are yourself; I might be anywhere."*

"That's not easy," Connie said, unable to stop herself.

"There's no time, Connie," the manager said. "Listen, here's the second:

> *"Long ago of use, now refuse—*
> *A needle, blade, or hook for fish, now rubbish.*
> *But when you're gone, we still hang on.*
> *We stick around, the last to go.*

"And the third:

> "*A world you don't see,*
> *A river you can't hear,*
> *More jewels and riches than any king—*
> *Travel far, I'm always near.*"

"Rubbish? A river you can't hear? I'm never going to get these," Connie said, discouraged. She looked into the manager's eyes. Something made her add, "But they're not too hard, really. I'm going to solve them. You've—you've really helped a lot."

The manager looked a little happier. "It's up to you and your brother now," she said.

"I know," Connie said. "We can do it. We never give up." She tried to sound as convincing as possible. Then she did something unexpected. Although she still felt shy, she stepped up to the manager and opened her arms.

Surprise came to the manager's face. Then she bent down and wrapped her thick arms around Connie.

"I guess it's allowed," she said.

She squeezed Connie very tight, so tight that Connie found it hard to breathe.

When the manager finally let go, Connie said to her, "We'll make it."

Connie opened her eyes.

❧

IT was dawn.

Sol had never gotten up from where he lay on his side beneath the ferns, changing. His knapsack still pressed against his back. He had called out Connie's name through the night. At first softly, as if worried someone besides Connie might hear him. Later loudly, without concern. His voice in the darkness had sounded, to his ears, strangled and strangely like an animal's. Later he'd fallen quiet. The thrush had stayed with him the whole night, flying off only twice—maybe to eat—and coming back soon after.

As the sky lightened and morning came, Sol opened his eyes and caught sight of the bird.

He said, "You—got to find—save her—even—you can't help—me." His voice croaked, almost barking. He found it hard to speak. He had to tense the muscles in his neck in directions that hurt to get any vowel sounds besides *eh*. He could feel his neck was long, and the muscles of his voice box seemed to be half absent. Moving his lips to make *mm* and *buh* sounds wasn't so hard, or getting the *kah* sound in the back of his throat for a *K* or *C*. The *T* sound he could do with the top of his long tongue. But *S* was very hard, and *R* seemed almost impossible.

"Connie—chance," he tried to say, hearing it come out like a growl. "She—sister." He hoped he sounded something close to what he meant.

He fell silent again.

The thrush hopped around him and fluttered up through the fern leaves. Dew dripped from the ferns onto Sol's fur. The thrush sang and, landing, pecked at the ground, seeming upset. Finally it took off, and after several minutes, Sol thought it wouldn't return.

He closed his eyes. These were his last moments. Like many kids, Sol had sometimes imagined a great— even if difficult—future for himself. How, when he grew up, he might think of a scientific theory that would help the world. The way his mother and others had discovered climate change. Sol might have done something important, because he was smart.

Now his future was changing as he changed. With each crack of a bone, it turned away from scientist toward beast. Maybe for some kids living one's life as an animal would be okay, better even than their actual lives. Maybe Theo was happy as an elk, like Sol remembered Monique had said.

But Sol could never be happy that way. Even if he could escape the hunter's arrows, the way Theo had.

He thought, I don't have to give up. Connie is out there somewhere.

Sol was sure of it. He couldn't imagine otherwise. She would be expecting him to do something. With an effort, he rolled over and stood on his four legs, breaking through the low ferns. Standing, they reached only to his deer knees, though they had hidden him totally when he'd been lying down. He trotted downhill toward the river. He stopped once to lower his head and feel his cheek with his front leg, in the motion most animals use to scratch. His head felt long, hard, and fur-covered.

Sol reached a field of high grass and wildflowers. The morning sky was clear, without clouds. Sol's eyes, as a deer, weren't strong like a human's. But he smelled the field well, every type of grass and flower, when he breathed in. He stretched his head forward and pulled at the wild grass with his mouth, chewing, swallowing, wondering, What can I do?

Then he knew. He still had the knapsack on, its

straps stretched out to full length. He felt them tugging tight in what used to be his armpits—his leg-pits now. He bent his front legs so that he was leaning on the ground on his front knees, his back legs standing. He lowered his head and shook the knapsack off over his head and his antlers. He had to shake hard, many times. After, he raised his head and pulled his front legs out of the straps one at a time. The knapsack lay in the tall grass.

Stepping on it to hold it down, he found the zipper with his mouth and unzipped it. His teeth were very strong. Once it was open, he stuck his head inside and started pulling things out with his mouth.

He pulled out his mother's scientific treatise and Holaderry's journal. Both were still a little wet from the river crossing yesterday. He pulled out the little blank notebook, then the paperback book he had packed, *The Mismeasure of Man*, though he was having trouble reading the words on the cover. He pulled out clothes—there was still a shirt and pants in there. Next came the pocketknife he'd found, rusted shut, the Valentine's Day card from his secret admirer—who he didn't think would admire him looking like he did now—and finally he reached what he wanted, his Know-It-All Cube that he'd built long ago and that Connie had somehow managed to ruin. He opened his mouth wide to get it between his jaws, and laid it in the grass.

"On," he said to it.

His voice croaked and sounded to his ears almost impossible to understand. It sounded more like an animal bleating "aw-mm" than like "on" to him.

But the cube understood, maybe because he had trained it using his own voice, and so it recognized Sol's manner of speaking better than anyone else's.

"Cube on," the cube said back in Sol's boy voice, which was strange for Sol to hear now.

Sol's first thought was: His waterproofing had held. He'd done a good job on that. The cube should have been shockproof too, though. It should never have crossed its circuits if all Connie had done was drop it. But life wasn't perfect. He'd learned that as a young scientist and inventor. Not everything he'd built worked just the way he hoped. There were always glitches and problems.

If only I can get it open, Sol thought now. He examined it with his deer eyes, sniffing it also. It was screwed together at the center of each edge, two halves held together by four screws—the slotted, single-groove kind.

Stepping on the cube with one front hoof, he took his other hoof and stuck it as hard as he could into the head of one of the screws. His hoof was thin at its end and flexible the way fingernails were flexible. He pushed hard, twisted, pushed hard and twisted.

And the screw turned a little! He did it some more, quickly, very hard. The screw turned easier each time. It rose and fell out.

Sol shouted, although his shout sounded like a bark.

He went on to the next screw, twisting with his hoof. It raised up with each turn and fell out. Then the next and the next. With four screws out, he was able to push the two halves of the cube apart and stare inside. It wasn't easy to see anything in the early morning light with his deer eyes. Still he saw the problem amid shadowy wires. The shockproofing *had* failed. When he'd built it long ago, the motherboard was held in the center by tiny plastic struts that gave if the cube was struck, absorbing the impact so the computer chips shook a little but never hit anything. But those struts hadn't worked. The motherboard had slipped loose from them and was stuck in the corner, with two side wires pulled out.

What did you do to it, Connie? he thought. Try to swat a fly with the cube? Bounce it like a tennis ball against the wall?

He pushed his long snout into the cube. It barely fit. He took hold of the loose wires with his big lips and used the end of his rough tongue to push them into the connectors. This was very difficult. He had to try a long time before it worked and the wires were in. He pulled his head away then.

"On," he barked, or something close to it. He had to tense the muscles in his neck painfully hard to do so and blow out with all his breath.

"I am on already," the cube said back in his voice, still understanding him.

"Menu," he worked hard to say, his throat feeling constricted.

It sounded to him like he had said *mehmoo*.

"Menu not available," his voice said back.

What to do now?

Think, Sol. But Sol was finding it hard to concentrate.

"System recover," he barked finally. It sounded to him like *sidem uhcuhva*.

But the cube understood him. "System recover on," the cube said back.

Sol had to remember. How did it go?

He tried to say, as slowly and clearly as possible, "Drive A, find . . . recover files . . . Configure, original configuration . . . ignore damaged files. Menu, select."

This is what he actually said—his throat straining, feeling a sharp pain in it as he did: "Dive ay fide . . . uhcuhva feil . . . cofiduh olidina cofiguladuh . . . ikno damag feil. Memoo, selet."

The cube hummed for a long time, then beeped and spoke, playing back words Sol had recorded long ago. "Reduced menu selected," it said. "Available programs: Encyclopedia mode, puzzle mode, math mode, coding mode."

It worked! Sol had been holding his breath and let out a grunt. The Know-It-All Cube wouldn't do everything. But some programs *would* run. Sol hoped that something somewhere in the cube might help Connie if she found it.

He trotted slowly down the field to the river. Sol shook his stubby tail without realizing it. He leaned down over the river and drank, lapping up the water with his rough tongue. The river flowed quietly here.

He didn't need to look to know that its currents were calm. He could close his eyes as he drank and tell where the currents were going by listening. He even heard, far upriver, a fish break the water's surface. Keeping his eyes closed and concentrating on the land behind him, he discovered that he could tell everything just from sound. He could tell how far away the trees behind the field were by the rustling of their leaves. He could hear the field by its silence, its lack of rustling, except for the whisper of wild grass.

He raised his deer head without opening his eyes then, nose up, and breathed in. Once, twice, then deeper. He could smell the river water and many plants from all directions. He caught each scent separately. If he breathed in several times, he could focus on one scent first and then, in a later breath, turn his mind to another, so that, by sniffing four or five times, he smelled everything around him: He smelled the river on the first breath; on the second breath, he focused on the scent across the river, which was harder; in the next one, he smelled the field, which was grass and flowers; in the fourth breath, the plants in the woods. He could even smell animals that were hiding in places in the brush.

And there were smells that lingered on after

something was gone. He smelled that a wolf had been near the river, though it was maybe several days past.

He opened his eyes.

The sky was bright, but the field wasn't as colorful as usual. Still, there were things out there past what he could see, things he could smell and hear. He could reach farther into the forest with those senses than with his sight.

This was the last part of his change, then. His brain itself was changing.

Everything beyond the forest—and the mountain peaks that he could see—was dropping out of his mind. It was like watching the sun set. Sol's memories were setting beyond where he could reach them. He was watching the memories sink away until he could only remember that he had once had memories, without knowing what they were.

His deer mind thought, *Now.*

Only now mattered.

He stamped hard on the ground and he leaped high. He flung his head this way and that on his powerful neck. He snorted and breathed in deeply, his nose in the air. He turned his ears to point in different directions so that he could hear what was out there.

Sol, as a boy, had always wished he were more athletic, stronger, faster, more coordinated. But never at the expense of his mind. He'd just wanted to be himself, but better. Now the kid who had built a Know-It-All Cube and a long-distance heat detection device, the best child scientist in his hometown, the smart brother who'd taught his younger sister many things, was gone.

He trotted across the field and reached a knapsack with things strewn around it. One of these was a book. Holding the book down with his hoof, he tore pages out of it, chewed, and swallowed.

He paused a long time sniffing an old yellowing treatise, then a leather journal, but he didn't eat either. He barked at a black plastic cube, lying open in two pieces. It didn't understand him and remained silent. He trotted on across the field, disappearing into the woods.

~~~

WHEN Connie awoke, she noticed immediately that her nose was stuffed. It reminded her at once of the morning before, when Sol had woken up with a high fever and headache because he was changing. Oh no, she thought, breathing in and finding her nostrils blocked. I'm sick too. I'm changing now too.

And at once the witch's words came to her—the words that had been in the back of her mind the whole time.

Hop along, Connie, after your brother!

Monique—whom Connie still thought of as the Camper Lady—had given Connie what Monique had called rabbit stew. Now Connie wondered, What if it was rabbit stew not because it had rabbit *in* it, but because it turned you into a rabbit when you ate it?

Had Monique eaten any?

No, Connie remembered.

Connie heard the rushing of the river and saw it through the trees. It was early morning. The sky was blue. It was the kind of day Connie had dreamed of when she'd imagined camping in the mountains, back in her hometown. She'd always wanted to go and live in nature, surrounded by mountain peaks. Now she just wanted a soft bed and to be safe with Sol.

She walked down to the river. Its water rushed by fast, rippling white. She got on her knees and leaned over to see herself. It was just her normal face looking back. But her ears . . . Connie had always had very large ears. The typical joke about her was that they were made that way so that everything she heard went in one ear and out the other. At least that's what

her father, Mr. Blink, used to say. Although sometimes he changed his comment to how her ears must
be blocked with wax instead.

"I'm wrong," he'd say. "It's not that everything I
say goes in one of your big ears and out the other. It's
that nothing ever makes it in, in the first place. They
must be blocked by wax and everything just bounces
off. *Bing.*"

Connie had always ignored his teasing, but she'd
secretly hoped that one day, as she grew, her head
might grow faster than her ears and so catch up with
them. Then they wouldn't look so big, sticking out to
the sides.

Now she stared at her reflection in the flowing
water, and she wondered if her ears weren't even
bigger than usual. They looked huge to her. But, she
thought, they had always been big.

It was so hard to tell!

Next, she wriggled her nose. Did it wriggle easier
than usual? But that was something she'd always been
able to do. She'd also always been able to touch the tip
of her nose with her tongue. She did both of those
sometimes to entertain people.

She gave up and sat back, trying not to think too

hard about it. She wasn't a rabbit yet—that's what was important. She could still fight on. And she had those riddles to solve. That was going to be tough. She didn't have a clue how to solve them. She had always been bad at riddles.

She wondered, If I solve the riddles, will Sol and I suddenly be taken out of the mountains? What exactly are they for? Then she thought of Sol. Well, she was always thinking of him, to tell the truth. Was he still half deer and half Sol? Had he become a full deer? If he was really a deer, did he have the mind of a deer, the intelligence of a deer? Was it up to her to save them both?

Connie had told the All Creatures manager that they would make it. But she'd said that mostly to make the manager feel better. Connie discovered that she didn't really have much hope. She and Sol had beaten Holaderry because they'd stuck together. But each of them alone, what chance did they have?

Connie tried to sniff in again but couldn't—her nose was totally blocked. She pulled some big leaves from a plant and blew her nose into them. It was messy, but she found it worked. She felt like a very primitive person doing that. She wiped her face with the leaves. This was the way people lived long ago, she thought.

She leaned down to the river water, cupped her hands, and drank with loud sips. She wasn't afraid that it was enchanted anymore. She had swallowed so much of the river water yesterday, she thought, it didn't matter. Maybe it *was* enchanted and she would turn into a deer, but also a rabbit. Then she'd become some sort of deformed woods monster, with giant rabbit feet and big horns—antlers, she corrected herself. Connie could imagine being that creature very well.

When she sat back, she saw a bird flying toward her.

CHAPTER

19

THE HUNT

MONIQUE LEANED OVER David's sleeping figure and sang,

> *Frère Jacques,*
> *Frère Jacques,*
> *Dormez-vous?*
> *Dormez-vous?*
> *Sonnez les matines,*
> *Sonnez les matines,*
> *Din dan don.*
> *Din dan don.*

David opened his eyes. What he saw was the witch looking not too old with her hair tied back in a pony-tail, her shirt with many pockets—a modern style very different from how she'd been dressed centuries ago, the first time he had seen her.

"I have sport for you," she said.

"I guessed," he answered. He made a spinning motion with his hand.

Monique understood at once and turned to face the wall. She heard him sliding out from his covers behind her and the squeak of the antique chest as it opened.

"What animal this time?" he asked.

"There are two," she said to the wall. "One is a deer. Sol, the older brother. He should have turned by now. The younger sister, Connie, won't have. I was late getting to her. I had to give her one of my stews. She should change this afternoon, though, and once she starts, it'll be fast. Twenty minutes, maybe. She's a wild rabbit."

Monique waited for a teasing remark about how she hadn't done a good job. She knew how much David hated it if the children weren't completely changed when she woke him. David was always grumbling about one thing or another.

He *belonged* on the evil side. She knew it. He belonged at *her* side. But David had never wanted to accept himself. No matter how many times she told him how easy cursing him had been. Three days, a few songs, a couple of potions fed to him in a fever, that was all it took to curse him for eternity.

Because he and his hunting party had been her partners all along.

Still, all David wanted to think about was the one afternoon he'd done something nice. As if he could balance a single good act against all the mischief he'd caused—a candle balanced against a forest fire.

Monique heard the antique chest close.

"Can I turn around now?" she asked.

"Yes," said David.

She turned. David was dressed in the same clothes he'd worn for hundreds of years—old-fashioned hunter's garb. A leather vest hung off his broad shoulders atop a white shirt with puffy sleeves. A flat cap was pulled down at an angle over his long, wavy locks. His leather pants were tied at his calves over woolen stockings, and on his feet were flat leather shoes.

David was very old, but he still looked like the young man he'd been when she'd first met him.

Monique bowed, sweeping her arm beneath her.

"Sire," she said.

"Very funny," David answered. "Okay, I can tell some things have gone wrong. Tell me everything I need to know to get these two. Since I *must*."

Monique wanted to say, Do you always have to complain when you ride off to do what you love most?

But she said instead, "They're being helped. Someone sent a wood thrush. I can guess who. A woman named Gertrude who lives in the town they came from, Grand Creek. The child-eating witch there, Fay Holaderry, took away most of Gertrude's power long ago. But something's happened to Fay, it seems, and Gertrude must have gotten at least some of her power back."

David's eyes met Monique's.

"How much does this Gertrude know?" he asked.

"It's impossible to tell," she said.

"Might she know what was left behind, or where?"

"She might," Monique admitted.

David almost smiled. *That* was the hunter Monique knew. The one who liked a challenge. Or was he hoping the children would get away? But he wasn't allowed to let them, and he was too skilled a hunter to fail.

"You really do have sport for me today," he said in a hard-to-read tone.

David bent down to walk through the doorway into the central room of the lodge. Monique went with him. Most of the animals of the lodge weren't looking at them as they entered. Only the opossum and the beaver watched the doorway to the bedroom.

The others were turned to stare at the chair by the hearth, or at the front door, or out the window.

David stepped to that window of cloudy glass now and put his face near it, looking out.

"A beautiful day," he said. He turned to her and held out his hand. "The possessions, please."

He meant things that belonged to the children. It was part of Monique's magic that David could sense when those he hunted were near, as long as he carried their possessions with him. Tracking down a lone animal in the woods would have been very difficult otherwise. Although this time was different. David already had an idea where the two children might be headed.

Monique drew Sol's socks out of her pocket, then the spoon that Connie had used to eat, and gave them to David.

"The spoon is for the girl, but she only used it a short time," Monique said. "I don't know how useful it will be."

David looked surprised but didn't say anything. He put the socks to his nose and sniffed. His eyes widened.

"The boy hasn't changed them in a while," he

said. "Are you sure you don't have anything of his that's a little less foul smelling?"

Monique shook her head no, even though she did have Sol's shirt and pants back at the cabin.

"Those will do," she answered.

David scrunched his lips and raised his cheeks in annoyance.

"Fine," he said. "Last sighting?"

"They left my cabin heading north, and I'm pretty sure they crossed the river beyond there. So, north and west."

"She knows," David said when he heard that. "Gertrude knows, and the wood thrush too."

"Maybe," Monique said.

"Makes the hunting easier, though, if I know where they're going."

"Don't worry. You won't have to chase after them for months like Theo."

David shook his head. "I don't know what you were thinking, turning that boy into an elk. It was like he was *born* to be one. Knew every way to avoid me. You did him a favor."

"Only because he escaped you," Monique said. "It wouldn't have been a favor if you'd felled him. Then he'd be here in this lodge."

David looked around at the still animals, each of them once a child.

"What a fate," he said, and it was impossible to know if he meant the children, or himself, or even Monique.

He took down his bow and quiver from where they hung on the wall. The bow went over his left shoulder, bowstring in front. He hung the quiver over his right shoulder. He could just feel the logbook against his back at the bottom of the quiver, below the arrows.

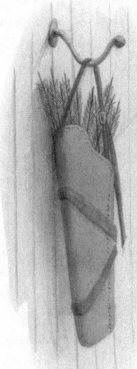

David pulled the front door open. Stepping through, he reached for his hunting horn overhead. He slid it into a loop on his belt.

The morning air was fresh. Downhill was his horse. He had no idea if Monique kept his old horse frozen still somewhere and revived him for David's hunts or if the horse had lived as long as David and simply grazed in some hidden part of the valley.

"Where *do* you keep him?" he asked, not for the first time.

"It's a secret—you know that," Monique answered. "You can't expect to know *everything* about my methods."

There were animals too that Monique sometimes took out of the lodge when the room became cramped—to make room for newer ones. She always said she was putting the animals "in storage." David didn't know where that was.

He walked down to untie his horse. Placing his foot in the stirrup, he gripped the saddle horn and mounted. Flicking the reins, he put his hand to his forehead, partly as a wave and partly a salute.

Monique stayed near the lodge doorway.

"Have fun!" she called as he disappeared into the trees.

❦

DAVID flicked the reins lightly, steering his horse only a little. His horse knew where they were going—to the ford over the river, where the horse had only to swim a few moments at the river's center before finding ground again and pulling them out of its currents.

David patted the horse on its neck.

"Where *does* she keep you, Tripper?" He'd started calling his horse by that name recently.

He had great sympathy for Tripper. He'd written once in his log, *If there's one thing worse than being a cursed hunter, it's being a cursed hunter's horse.*

Once across the ford, David shortened the reins to steer Tripper crashing through trees where they both had to watch their heads. Tripper snorted, walking them uphill through thick growth for more than a mile, until they finally reached a plateau of evergreen trees with more space. Then Tripper broke into a canter.

It was a perfect day for the hunt. The sun hadn't risen high enough to escape over the eastern mountain peaks, but the blue sky was already bright and clear. That was something about the accursed valley—days seemed short since the sun broke free of the eastern mountains only late in the morning, crossed the sky, and quickly fell behind the high western mountains by mid-afternoon.

David took his horn from his belt and raised it to his lips. He blew as hard as he could. Its blast carried across the valley. Right then, he heard a crashing in the brush ahead.

He knew it couldn't be the boy or girl, Sol and Connie, Monique had called them. He was nowhere near where they would be now. Still he spurred Tripper on, and soon, at a gallop, he caught sight of a big female deer running ahead, dodging, making so much noise that David could hear it even over Tripper's *clippety-clop*. He steered Tripper to cut in ahead of the deer's path. The deer caught sight of them, too late, and tried to turn back. By then Tripper was very close upon it—close enough that David could see the white markings on the gray deer's shoulders.

He drew an arrow in a split second and nocked it in his bow while Tripper galloped. David held on to the jolting horse with his legs only, took sight of the deer, raised his bow, aimed, and . . . didn't fire.

David was just warming up. He eased the bowstring forward, still holding it, until he could take his arrow out. Pulling Tripper back to a canter, he rode on.

CHAPTER

REUNITED

THE THRUSH FLEW LOW over the river toward Connie, following the river's curve. Connie wasn't sure at first if it was just a normal bird. But it landed in front of her.

Right then, Connie heard something that chilled her to the bone. It sounded almost like an elephant trumpeting far off in the woods. But it wasn't that, she knew. It was the blast of an old-fashioned hunting horn. The hunt was on.

The thrush called out melodies that ended in chattering noises.

"Where's Sol?" Connie asked.

The bird lowered its head, pulled in its wings, and ran in one direction and then another, head down. The thrush was trying to tell Connie something, but it was hard for her to know exactly what. It took off downriver then, and Connie followed. The bird flew beside the riverbank. Connie kept up as best she could, climbing over gnarly roots and through mud.

Then, at one point, the thrush flew over the river.

"I can't swim across, bird," she called to it.

Connie found that she had a terrible fear of swimming in that river. Despite the fact that its waters were slower here. If she'd had adults with her—if it had been before she'd been swept away in its currents—she wouldn't have thought too much about swimming across.

But now she knew how dangerous a river could be, even a lazy, calm-looking one. Her chest grew tight just at the thought of going in.

The thrush stood on the other bank, singing, and it didn't come back. It flew a bit farther on, to something lying in a field. It was hard for Connie to see through the wild grass on the other side, but from the thing's color, red, and the way it lay, she thought she knew what it was: Sol's pack.

If she was going to go after Sol, she had no choice. She *had* to cross that river. Nothing else in the wide world would have made her splash into the cold river water in her jumper and shoes. For a long time, she was able to walk, until it was finally up to her waist. Her heart pounded. And then she dove forward, not just into the river's current but, it felt like, into her fear. That fear overwhelmed her as the water covered her. She felt herself moving in the current as she swam, but gently. She stroked and stroked. She was making headway. And before she knew it, she was standing again, splashing out on the other side.

She hadn't conquered her fear exactly. But she had faced it and won.

She walked out into the high grass, bedraggled and wet. She reached the red knapsack. It was unzipped. Holaderry's journal lay in the grass next to it. The pages were wavy from getting wet and drying. Her Valentine's Day card lay next to it. Connie had never told Sol the truth about the card, which made her feel bad. Their mother's final scientific treatise was there too. It had already blown away a little.

Sol would never have left that behind, thought Connie. It was the most important thing in the world to him. Unless he'd been caught, or if he really was a deer now. That was when Connie found the paper-back book, *The Mismeasure of Man*, chewed to pieces. Another animal might have passed by and done that, but Connie began to suspect that Sol was a deer. Also, the hunter's horn had sounded far off. Sol couldn't be caught yet.

Sol's spare clothes were spread on the ground, and the rusty knife they had found too. Finally, Connie discovered the cube lying between violet wild-flowers. The cube had fallen apart, or so it looked to Connie. Its top half hung off the bottom half with wires stretched between.

She picked up the knapsack. The only thing that was still in there was the empty water bottle and, under it, a pencil. She collected all the items from the ground and put them back in. She missed the little blank notebook so that was left to lie in the field.

"Sol!" she called, at first not at her absolute loud-est. But then she shouted loudly, screaming into the valley.

"Sol! Sol!"

She kept hoping to see a deer come out of the woods. What would Sol look like as a deer? Would she even recognize him? She thought she would.

No one came, though.

The last thing she put into the knapsack was the cube. She laid the knapsack on the ground, open, and picked the cube up carefully, cradling the two halves with both hands.

A lot of things ran through her mind then, not least a memory of when, what seemed like long ago, maybe more than a year, she had snuck into Sol's room and taught the cube to say nice things about her. Quantum had startled her back then. He'd snuck into the room with her and jumped on her arm, using his claws to hang on to her sleeve. Quantum was always jealous if she paid attention to other things, and she had been talking to the cube long enough, Quantum had decided. Connie had dropped the cube then, and it hadn't just fallen—it had struck the corner of Sol's bed leg hard and tumbled to the floor, rolling like a giant die.

She'd been afraid that she'd broken it and left quickly after putting the cube back where she'd found it. She had never heard about the cube later, though, so she thought it had still worked after all. She hadn't realized that Sol hadn't used the cube afterward—that he'd long since become bored with that invention and moved on to more complex devices.

The two halves, connected by wires, were by her lips now as she put it into the knapsack. She wished to hear it say anything in Sol's voice, even if it was just Connie mode.

"On," she said to it, not expecting an answer, since it looked so broken.

"I am on already," it said in Sol's voice, so low that she could hardly hear it.

That surprised her completely.

"Menu," she said to it.

"Reduced menu selected," it said back weakly in Sol's voice. "Encyclopedia mode, puzzle mode, math mode—"

"Stop," Connie said.

"Stopped," Sol's voice said back.

Connie had never heard it say *reduced menu* before. Something had changed. She thought for a moment and tried, "Encyclopedia mode."

"Encyclopedia mode selected, speak entry," Sol's voice said quietly.

"Sol, you fixed it!" Connie cried out.

The cube heard her and started: "*Sol*, Latin for

sun. Also, short for Solomon, as in King Solomon or Solomon Blink, my inventor."

"I can't believe it," Connie said. "You fixed it, Sol."

The cube said in Sol's voice, "I do not understand. Please speak your entry again slowly and clearly."

"Deer," she said.

"*Dear*," Sol's voice said weakly from the cube, "highly valued, precious, also expensive. Used as a synonym for sweetheart and honey. Also, *deer*, any mammal belonging to the family Cervidae, including roe deer, white-tailed deer, moose, elk, and caribou."

Wow, Connie thought, it really did know everything. But most important, it was just nice to hear Sol's voice.

The thrush landed on the knapsack, which folded under its weight. It called and tweeted.

"Okay, I'm hurrying," Connie said, although she hadn't been.

She was about to put the cube into the knapsack carefully when a glint in the grass caught her eye. It was a screw. She found two others. Those were from the cube. She was able to put them into the holes along the edges of each half of the cube, lining the holes up. She turned the screws enough to hold the cube together.

The bird was singing loudly.

"I'm done," she said to it.

She packed the cube, zipped up the knapsack, put it on her shoulders, shortened the straps so it fit her, and said, "Okay, lead on, bird. Let's go find Sol."

PLUG ME IN

BUT WERE THEY GOING to go find Sol? The little thrush had a critical decision to make. It had heard the hunter's horn. It knew the lay of the land and how fast the hunter could travel on a horse. It could guess how long they had before the hunter would ride up on them—not long.

It also knew the direction Sol had gone in. It had searched while Connie was packing and found Sol's trail headed in the wrong direction—due west rather than northwest. If the thrush took Connie that way, the hunter would ride up behind them, probably before they even found Sol, and their escape path would be cut off. Both children would be caught by the hunter.

There *was* still a chance, though, for Connie. If they went directly for the mountain pass, they might make it. Especially if the hunter rode after Sol instead of them.

But that meant leaving Sol behind. The decision was too big for a little thrush to make alone. While Connie had been packing up, the bird had cried out for the All Creatures manager, hoping that it might be heard even this far off, and sense the manager responding in its mind, telling it what to do.

But no answer had come. The thrush flew up to the topmost branch of a tree, looking over the woods west, then to the peak northwest—not so far.

What to do?

The thrush was supposed to save both children. Not just one.

That had been its great errand.

This decision shouldn't have been up to it alone.

But it was.

The thrush had to decide.

Save one. Or lose both.

⁓⸎⁓

CONNIE followed the bird on a hard route uphill. They were headed toward the mountain she had seen two days ago from up on the ledge, the one with the crescent-shaped peak.

"Sol!" she called out once in a while.

She heard sounds in the forest, hidden animals moving, just rustling in low leaves running away from her and the bird. The sun had finally escaped over a mountain peak into the sky, and it was warmer. Overhead, when she looked up, a hawk circled in the air.

Connie faced up to a hard truth, that she *was* a sister who always messed Sol's stuff up. She *did* sneak into his room and take things out that she wasn't supposed to. And she liked to play tricks on Sol too, it was true—if only to prove that he wasn't the only smart one. Sol thought he was a genius. He *was* a genius. But she was smart too.

No, that wasn't the point of what she should be thinking now. What she was trying to think was, If she hadn't messed up Sol's know-everything cube, they would be out of here by now. Instead Sol was a deer and a hunter was coming after them. That hunter would freeze Sol with an arrow, *whack*, in the head or maybe in the chest. Sol had tried to protect her by drinking the water first, and that's why he was in danger. And, back in Grand Creek, when she had been caught by Holaderry, Sol had come to save her.

Everything, she saw, was her fault. But, fighting

against that idea, she thought, Sol's done wrong things too. *Everyone* does wrong things. It's okay to make mistakes. It was just like adults always told her; everyone made mistakes.

Well, now it's my turn, she thought. I'm going after Sol, and I'll save him somehow. No more mistakes, no more secrets.

This was her moment. But even as she thought this, half running clumsily down a hill after the bird, she heard Sol's voice from the knapsack and stopped running immediately. She shook the knapsack off and took the cube out.

"Battery low," the cube said weakly in Sol's voice. "Plug me in. Warning. Battery low."

Oh no, she thought. She had forgotten to turn it off, and it had probably been low on batteries already.

"Off," she said to it. "Turn off."

"Off," the cube said quietly.

"Are you off?" she asked it.

It didn't reply.

She sat down. And that was when she thought of it. Maybe they had a chance after all.

She wondered if it was possible.

"On," she said to the cube.

"Cube on," it said very quietly in Sol's voice. "Battery low. Plug me in. Warning. Battery low."

It stopped.

"Menu," she said.

"Reduced menu selected," Sol's voice said back, very low. "Encyclopedia mode, puzzle mode, math mode—"

"Riddles," Connie said. "Can you solve riddles?"

"Puzzle mode selected. Crosswords and synonyms. Anagrams. Riddles—"

"Riddles!"

"Riddle mode selected," it said. "Battery low. Plug me in. Warning. Battery low." It paused. "Please state riddle."

Connie knew that people can do incredible things when it's very important—like lifting cars with their bare hands. She had seen that on a video. And even me, she thought happily. Because she had memorized all three riddles. She knew it. Because if she *had* forgotten them, she realized, she would never have forgiven herself.

She took a deep breath and recited what she could remember, *"I am called what you are called. With you a lot I share. But when I—I mean you—but when you in a mirror stare, I am not there, I could be anywhere."*

"Finished?" Sol's voice asked from the cube.

"Finished."

"Computing. Sometimes called what you are called," it said. "This can mean things in the same category. Example: chair, table, bed—all called *furniture*. Rose, weed, poison ivy—all called *plant*."

"No, I don't think that's right," Connie said. "This shares something with me. It's called what I am called."

Suddenly, it came to Connie.

"Off," she said.

"Off," the cube said back.

"Are you off?"

No answer.

Sometimes called what she was called, Connie thought.

A girl? A kid? Connie?

No, she didn't think the riddle meant *her*, specifically, when it said *what you are called*. Usually riddles were for everyone. But, she thought, a family name. That was shared by everyone in a family. A mother, a father, a brother, a sister, even cousins, aunts, and uncles were sometimes called the same: by their last name!

The answer to the riddle *called what you are called* was someone in your family. Connie was almost sure of it. A brother or sister or mother or father. It fit the rest of the riddle too. They shared a lot with you, and when you looked in a mirror they could be anywhere.

"I've got it," she said to the cube.

It didn't answer.

"On," she said.

"Cube on. Battery low. Plug me in. Warning. Battery low."

"I know," she said. "Riddles, I mean puzzles."

"Puzzle mode selected. Cross—"

"Riddles."

"Riddle mode selected," it said. Its voice was very low now. "Please state riddle."

"*Long ago of use*," Connie recited. This was a hard one. "*Now reh–fuse. A needle, or fishing hook, hook for fish, now rub–bish. But when you're gone, we hang on. We stick around, the last to go.*"

"Finished?" the cube asked.

"Finished."

"Battery very low. Warning." It paused. "Of use. A needle or hook. This could mean a building material. Suggestions: metal, wood, stone, plastic. Ten seconds," it said. "Shutting down. Nine, eight, seven—"

"No!" Connie said. "Stop! Off. Off."

"Off," the cube said weakly.

"Are you off?"

No answer.

It was enough to make Connie cry. She had waited too long, the cube had been on too long, she had forgotten to turn it off when she'd packed it, and she hadn't solved the riddles. She wasn't doing a good job of saving Sol.

CHAPTER

22

WHAT WAS LEFT BEHIND

MEANWHILE, SOL THE DEER had run from the river west until reaching a field of reeds that grew in grassy mud and water—a marsh. Smelling and listening, he'd waded into the mud, which, as he went onward, became a reed-filled pond. His long, thin legs sank into the unseen mud underwater until the pond water rose and reached halfway up his body, almost to his tail. Reeds blocked his view in every direction. Very slowly, he pulled himself through the pond.

Then the hunter's horn blast sounded from far off, striking fear into his heart. But he couldn't move fast. He tried to walk faster, but that only made his legs sink into the mud more, which made him struggle more. Until the water covered his back, reaching up his neck, and he felt the mud underwater touch his belly—that was the bottom of the pond. His legs were completely sunk in the ground.

He stopped and stood still, more afraid of sinking deeper now than he was afraid of the hunter—whom his deer mind envisioned as a kind of giant, cruel, smart animal. Only his head was out of the pond's water. Gnats and flies found him and began buzzing around his head, zooming over the water and landing on his antlers, his mouth, and his eyes. He shook his head hard so that they took off, but they landed again a second later.

His legs were so deep in the earth that he couldn't pull them out anymore. But he was able to lift them high enough to force them forward through the mud, a little each time. Like that, he inched incredibly slowly through the pond, making little waves in the water around him. The bugs annoyed him, driving him crazy. They landed on his thick lips and his eyes. He shook his head violently to no avail.

The marsh pond wasn't wide, but it took so long to cross it, the sun had moved in the sky before he reached the other side. At last he pulled himself up onto solid, if wet, land. Ahead was a deep wood of shadows. The marsh reeds were behind him.

He trotted between the trees. He heard something moving, raised his snout, and breathed in, smelling the scent. A few careful steps forward, and he saw a huge elk.

The elk was watching him. It had already heard him. It shook its head in a powerful swing and ran off—not fast, but fast enough. Sol the deer watched.

At last, he sprang after it, due west, running farther and farther away from the mountain pass.

❧

GERTRUDE set Lenore's letter on the kitchen table. She was upstairs over her shop in the kitchen past her bedroom, where the windows looked down on the street. She put a teakettle on the stove and gazed out. A woman walked by. Soon after, the kettle whistled, its whistle quickly rising to a shriek. She turned it off. The kettle's shriek sank to a thin cry, then silence. She poured the steaming hot water into a ceramic teapot with loose tea leaves at its bottom. She put the teapot lid on with a click, and sat at the kitchen table.

There was nothing to do now but wait.

Gertrude could give no more hints, tell no more riddles, send no more help than she already had. Holaderry had gotten the best of her ages ago and, though Gertrude could do a little more now, she was still weak. For how much longer? Another hundred years?

She unfolded Lenore's letter. She'd brought it up from the cellar library to read once more—to lose herself in the distant past.

She remembered when she and Lenore had been girls together, centuries ago. Not close friends, but they had recognized each other as different from those around them. Powerful. In those days, having powers was extremely dangerous. People feared witchcraft and grabbed hold of anyone they suspected, dealing them the ultimate punishment. It drew children like Gertrude and Lenore together. Whenever they had seen each other, they exchanged knowing glances. Gertrude well remembered Lenore's sturdy frame and her piercing stare.

Gertrude had once met a third girl with powers, who had seemed nice, but had grown up to be an evil witch.

Not Lenore, though.

Gertrude lifted the lid of the teapot. The tea was ready. She poured it into a cup. Its comforting aroma reached her nose. She held the letter far to her left.

She was a bit clumsy and likely to spill tea on it no matter how careful she tried to be.

She lifted the cup to her lips and blew.

She read:

To my friend Gertrude,

I have written this letter to you many times over. Maybe this is the one I will finally send. I have to tell you. I have to tell someone, someone who knows, who knew my little brother, Fauntleroy. Someone who will care.

He has died, and I feel it is my fault. Can you imagine what that feeling is like?

You would say it is not my fault. But I am the one who decided to take him with me. I couldn't imagine leaving him behind. I thought I could take care of my brother, watch over him. I never realized what we would face on the road that lay ahead of us. I felt confident of my powers and of his. But he was too young. I should have gone alone, even if it split us up, even if it meant we would never see each other again. Even if it meant leaving him with our awful father.

You remember how it was for us. Our parents were so despicable. They had everything, their estate, their servants, their wealth, but none of it mattered. You remember the day I cooked soup myself for my family, brought it to them, and my stepmother, when she tasted it, said it was awful and threw the hot soup in my face. You remember how badly it burned me. You saw the blisters.

And Fauntleroy, he acted just like the boy he was, playing, fooling, and Father beat him for the annoyance. No one helped us. They were afraid to offend our parents. Well, there were servants who helped.

And then there was the affair with Miss Rosaline from town. I am sure you remember that well. They said she had powers. They called her a witch, although she wasn't. She had no more power than watchful eyes. She was an ordinary woman, yet they dragged her away, banished her forever. I thought, That will be me and Fauntleroy next. You told me once, when we talked in town, remember? You said it was only a matter of time before our special powers were discovered. My parents would have given me and Fauntleroy to the townspeople without hesitation.

I should have written you before we left. We would have had more chance all together. But it was a quick decision. When I heard my parents' carriage clatter away, I told Fauntleroy,

—We're going.

We loosed the other horse so that they would think we took it on the road. A stable boy helped me with that, although it could cause trouble for him. I hope he was okay. Then I took us on the only trail no one would suspect, over the mountaintop and through the accursed woods.

I knew the stories were true, that there was a curse on that valley and a witch who lived there. I thought we were powerful enough, not to beat her but to avoid her. One day of hiking was all we needed, and we would have been past and far from home. But it took all afternoon and into the night to climb the mountain by the rock waterway and to cross into the valley. We slept high up that first night. We went on at dawn's light. We finished our water, but there are always streams to drink from in the woods.

When we stopped at the first brook, though, I heard it whispering to me,

—Whoever drinks from me will become a tiger.

And the second we found said,

—Whoever drinks from me will become a wolf.

Fauntleroy didn't hear it. His powers were different, he could turn people's thoughts in odd directions, you remember. But he didn't feel for nature the way you or I did. I told him what I'd heard, and to make it more serious for him, because he was so young, I told him,

—If you drink from these streams, you will turn into a vicious animal and hurt me.

That made him stop, although I saw thirst in his eyes.

At the third stream, I heard,

—Whoever drinks from me will become a roe deer.

He asked me what it said then, and I told him. He kept staring at the water and licking his lips. Then suddenly he drank before I could stop him. He sat back up and said,

—I won't hurt you if I become a deer. See? And I'm fine anyway. The stream's lying.

Silly Fauntleroy! He started to change, and it didn't take long. I pulled a ribbon from my hair, tied it around his deer neck, and kept him with me. But when hunters in the valley blew their loud horns, he took fright. He ran off…

Gertrude sipped her tea, skimming through the part about Fauntleroy coming back as a wounded

deer and how the hunter had ridden up and helped them. Lenore thought it was Fauntleroy's power to change minds that had turned the hunter's shot and convinced the hunter to take them out. Even as a deer, perhaps in extreme panic, his power had shone through. Gertrude herself wasn't so sure.

It's all over, Gertrude thought. It happened so long ago. Gertrude was one of those people who thought there was strength in acceptance, instead of in strong feeling. She read on for the part that concerned her now, the part after Lenore and her brother left the hunter behind and crossed the pass.

Lenore wrote:

We reached the mountain pass and crossed it, climbing down the rocks. Fauntleroy was badly wounded, and his wound had opened more during the ride. I was already ahead when he did what many a hurt animal will do. He found a place to hide. We passed a small cave, and Fauntleroy stopped. He looked at me with his deer eyes, hesitated, and limped into the cave.

Inside, he lay down full on his side, with his four long legs stretched out before him. His chest rose and fell with each loud breath that he blew through his snout. I kneeled beside, leaned over him. Gertrude, my tears fell on my brother but disappeared at once in his deer fur. I put my hands on his chest, and my hands rose and fell with each breath too, until they didn't anymore. Fauntleroy was still.

How I wept.

I learned my lesson at a terrible cost, Gertrude. The world is a big place, and there is more in it than we imagined, and we are not as strong as we think. I have gone where no one can follow. I dream of revenge, but I know that dream will darken my future, not lighten it. I cannot take revenge on the whole world.

Gertrude, I don't know if my spell worked, but before I left that cave, I tried one.

Gertrude read of the spell Lenore had woven then, hoping that it had indeed worked. It was Sol and Connie's chance, if only they knew what to do. She finished the letter and her tea too with a gulp.

I am safe and sound and your friend,
    Lenore

CHAPTER

23

SEVEN HUNTERS

DAVID BITTWORTH JUDGED that he and Tripper had gone far enough. He steered Tripper back to the river. There, he thought, he should pick up the trail. He put Sol's stinky socks to his nose and breathed in deeply. The smell tightened David's stomach in a way that told him he was closing in on the boy. He took out the spoon next and gripped it in his fist, trying to sense Connie, but got no feeling from it. He didn't know if that was because the spoon had little connection to her, or if she was farther away.

Tripper trotted through a grove of willow trees and across a hill of ferns. They came into a field of high grass and wildflowers. David dismounted.

"That way," he said to Tripper, pushing the horse to one side. "Don't destroy the evidence."

The kids had been here. He could feel it. The boy or both of them. He walked along the southern verge of the field. South is where they would have come from. Other animals had crossed this field too, of course. The children wouldn't be the only ones. But their trail should be new, possibly just a few hours old. David could tell recent trails from older ones, since the bent wild grass straightened slowly over days. He found one trail from the morning, he estimated. The high grass was all the way down and had come up only a little.

This would most likely be theirs. He followed the path, looking by the grass roots for prints. He noticed wildflowers whose tops were bitten off. The boy then, if this was his trail, was a deer already. Knowing that, he crouched down, pushed the grass aside, and found a hoofprint. That print was no more than the faintest curve in the earth, but David would have recognized a hoofprint like that anywhere.

What about the girl? Where were her prints? The trail led to a place that had been trampled completely in the middle of the field. It looked as if something had been laid down on the grass. He found the edge of a shoe print. A small size. So, the girl Connie had been here, and she had still been a girl. Next he found a little notebook. He paged through it. It was blank. Then he noticed something shiny on the ground. He picked it up carefully. A screw.

Odd, David thought.

From here, a trail of bent wild grass went down to the river. He thought it led away from this area to the water. But he discovered there were two paths. One went the straightest way to the riverbank, and the grass on that one was bent down pointing toward the river, so whoever had made it was headed to the river just like he thought. It was narrow, and flower heads had been bitten off along the path. The boy, Sol. The deer. The other path had grass that was bent away from the river and into the field. It was wider. He found the slight mark of a shoe heel in the middle of this path. The girl, Connie. She had walked *from* the river. He reached where that path began at the water and stared over to the opposite bank.

The river wasn't fast here.

She had swum across.

They'd been separated.

He went back to the central, trampled area. What had happened, he wondered, and where had they

gone next? The other paths were less obvious because on the northern part of the field the grass was
broken up around rocks. But for David, they weren't
hard to find. Again, two paths.

That surprised him. They hadn't met here and
gone off together. One narrow trail led into the
woods away from the river. West. More chewed high
grass. The boy.

A second, wider trail—the girl—stayed close to the
river, toward a steep climb. Northwest.

Now David had to think like the ancient hunter
he was. Monique had said there was a bird helping the
children, sent by a woman in Grand Creek. Gertrude,
he remembered. David imagined her back in town,
another long-lived person like him and Monique. He
wondered what she looked like and, especially, how
much she knew. She had sent the children help. Did
that mean she knew exactly how to help them and
where to lead them? David had to assume that she
did. That fact was in his favor, though, since the bird
had shown itself. He knew now that the children were
being led somewhere, and he could guess where.

They were headed for the pass. He could get
ahead of them and cut them off.

But here was a new puzzle. The girl's trail continued in the direction he thought they must be heading, while the boy's trail led off in the wrong direction, toward a wide marsh.

They hadn't been together, David knew that. The bird, then, was leading the girl. And the boy, who had passed here first, had gone off in the wrong direction. The bird had had to make a quick decision, David saw. Follow the boy west toward what David knew was marshland, but then David would have caught all three of them. They would have had no route to escape. Or the bird could lead the girl to the pass and hope to reach it before David did, splitting up the brother and sister. Lose the boy to save the girl.

It's not easy being the leader, is it, bird? David thought. *I was leader once too.*

David had to make his own decision now. Go after the boy and let the girl reach the pass and escape the valley, or ride after the girl, get her, and then her brother afterward—*or*, he thought, *at the same time.*

⁕

DAVID was sure that he knew where Connie was being led. Still, he tried to use the spoon Monique had given him. But it was really no help at all. Connie must have held it for only a short time. He gripped it in his fist as he rode. He put it to his nose—it smelled faintly of stew. He pressed it to his forehead, and still he felt nothing. So, after riding for close to half an hour, he dismounted and looked for tracks. He crouched, leaning forward on the tips of his toes, his head and shoulders bent over the ground. He almost fell forward but regained his balance. He looked left and right by moving his eyes only. He tilted his head next so that one ear pointed toward the ground and the other aimed into the air. Then, using his intuition, he took a few steps past a high bush between gray-barked trees—young pines—and leaned over where the ground was moist. There he found what he was looking for—a footprint.

He mounted Tripper and rode on. He came to the longest field in all the valley. Gazing across, he saw far off in the distance what he knew he would.

Seven horses with seven riders, frozen still. This was the field where Monique, in a cloud of darkness that had stretched over the trees, had stopped David and his hunting party.

He galloped across and reached them. His seven friends still had their bows on their shoulders and their horns on their belts. Their faces were frozen in looks of fear. Of course. They had been watching the dark shadow rise over them. Two of the horses had been frozen with mouths open and lips pulled back—huge, block teeth showing.

David knew that if he reached over and touched one of the men or horses, the skin would feel soft, like normal skin. He'd done it before. They weren't stone statues or frozen like ice. They were preserved the same way the animals of the lodge were preserved, stopped forever at a moment in time.

David steered Tripper between them, recalling what his friends had been like. He remembered especially how they had cheered for him.

Hurrah!

The good old days.

He turned at last to gaze past the field where, above the trees, a mountain peak loomed close against the sky in the shape of a gigantic pickax. At least that's what David thought the peak looked like; others said it was a crescent like the moon.

The bird was leading the girl to that peak. This was the path David had ridden centuries ago with that other girl and her brother the deer, his whole hunting party following him until this field. Connie and the bird would have crossed here hours ago.

Was it possible for them to climb the mountain and reach the pass before he arrived?

He didn't think so. Still, they had one advantage. They could go straight. He didn't want them to hear or see him, however, so he had to ride in a wide arc. North, he decided. It was clearer for riding, a rocky, grassy land of spruce trees. But the eastern face of the mountainside was terrible for hiking. He'd have to leave Tripper behind, climb cliffs, and cross two wide, roaring brooks.

He waved goodbye to his old friends. He rode hard for an hour or so and reached the place where he had to leave Tripper, by a rocky gorge. From Tripper's saddlebag, he took ropes and the knife that he needed.

He said goodbye to his horse. Tripper was happy to be released. The horse would wander near the base of the mountain until David came looking for him.

The route up the eastern face of the mountain was worse than David remembered, especially carrying the ropes, knife, and his bow and quiver. One rocky climb in particular was steep and difficult. He pulled himself up a sheer rock face, clutching with his fingers. The ropes on his shoulder pushed him away from the rock, which made it harder. Once a stone under his foot came loose and fell. It made several *clacks* as it bounced down the rock face. He was sure that could be heard for miles. Would the girl hear it?

But when he reached a level shelf that led into the woods again, he had a southern view of the mountainside below and saw her—a tiny figure crossing an open patch before she disappeared into the trees again. She was on the most direct climb to the mountain pass.

It would take her a while to reach where he was. David had some time. He slid the ropes off his shoulder, then his quiver. He took the arrows out of the quiver, reached in, and felt his logbook and pencil. He pulled them out. He sat, his back against a tree, opened the log, and wrote:

Monique says that I was always a villain, even if I never wanted to face that fact as a young man. She says I knew in my heart what I was hunting, but I ignored my intuition because I cared more about myself than the children. I loved showing off for the townspeople, she reminds me. I loved proving how brave I was, riding into the accursed valley. I loved leading my friends, being called the king. I loved their cheers.

I loved proving how skilled a hunter I was. Bringing back felled game. Being the best.

If that meant ignoring hints and feelings about what I was hunting, ignoring warnings—even those shouted at me by an old fortune-teller—then so it was.

Monique says I thought I could live like a villain but be honored as a hero.

Yes. Yes. Yes, I always respond. I know it, don't I? I'm not the only one.

But she took advantage of my situation.

The strangest thing for me is her punishment for the choices I made as a young man—my curse: that I must continue to do what I loved to do, ride through this valley and hunt, using my skills as a horseman and an archer.

Of course I no longer get to hear the cheers of my friends or see awe in the eyes of the townspeople. But I still get to ride.

Monique says I should thank her for that. I can spend an eternity doing what I love best.

But there is a difference between then and now: I can no longer pretend to myself, or to others, that I don't know what it is I do or who it is I am. I've tried to tell her that ruins all the fun.

Someday, maybe, a young man or woman will read this log of mine. Then I have this to say to you: If you suspect even a little that you might be a villain like me, but you are still pretending to yourself or to others not to be, think twice about what you are doing. Even if everyone around you cheers. Even if the townspeople shower you with fortune or fame. Even if they pin medals to your chest. Think three times. Four times. A hundred times! Listen to the whispers deep inside of you. There's a chance to change your destiny.

My curse is that I cannot change. In a way, I am as frozen in time as my friends and their horses in the great field.

There are rules to my curse: I must always try my hardest, just as I did when I was a young hunter. I must use ALL my skills as a hunter, a horseman, and an archer. I cannot turn my shot or hesitate. I cannot ride too slowly or sneeze when I'm hiding out to ambush an animal. And, just for example, if there are two children in these woods, I cannot let one go if I have the chance to catch both. (Sorry, Connie.)

This is why children have no chance against me. I

*was always the best hunter of all, and I am still the best.
You must simply try, children, to stay out of these accursed woods. Or, if you are on the run, get through
them quickly and drink from no stream.*

*Monique is right. She just turns the children to
animals.*

I am the one who decided what to do with them.

There is a monster in these woods, and it is me.

David stopped writing.

He needed time to fashion his traps.

Using his knife, he cut off branches from young
evergreens. Many crows were here in the trees, watching as usual. Whenever there was any action in the
accursed valley, the crows gathered. David thought,
They don't want to miss the big finale. There were
hundreds of them, lined up until the very last trees of
the mountain before the treeline ended at the rocky
land of the pass. They were cawing loudly at each
other and at him.

"Be quiet," he told them in a low voice.

But the crows never listened to him or to anyone.

He found logs that he positioned along the open
part of the path where the girl Connie would choose

to walk, he was sure. Those logs would steer her in the right direction. He tied his rope to a tree trunk, tossed its end over a sturdy limb, measured out a length, and cut the rope by bending it around his knife blade. That end he tied into the trap and hid, as best he could, beneath plants that grew close to the ground. He hoped to make five such traps before she came into sight.

But as he was hiding his third, he heard the cracking of branches from below. It was so loud no animal could have made such a commotion, besides the animal called *human*. But of course the girl was tired. He stepped carefully through brush to hide behind a very wide tree. Only then did he realize that he'd left the rest of his rope behind, lying curled up by a tree trunk but in plain sight if the girl looked in the right direction.

It was too late to get it. He saw her now, Connie, wasting a lot of energy winding left and right as she climbed. A little brown thrush flew next to her. She wore a red knapsack. What was most striking about her were her ears. They'd grown higher than her head and pointy at their tops. She was very short too. Her change had begun.

Besides that, David was struck by Connie's clothes and her hairstyle—her hair was short like a boy's. Was that a new style for girls? It was very rare that David saw the children he hunted while they were still children. He hated when that happened.

Even David's curse couldn't force him to hunt children who were still children. But there were a few over the centuries who hadn't changed in time, like Connie, even while he hunted their friends or siblings. In that case, it was David's job simply to keep them in the valley until they completed their transformation. But those children had been only a handful over hundreds of years.

As Connie drew nearer, he studied her. Her cheeks were wide. Her lips were thin. He thought she looked capable for her age. She kept stopping and looking ahead, then starting again. He ducked back each time. She reached the first log that he'd pulled across the open land.

This was the moment of truth. If she jumped up on the log and over, she might miss the trap and even the others ahead. But, David was glad to see, she was too tired. She turned and walked around the log, which put her feet just steps from the hidden loop of rope.

Still, she had luck and walked by it.

Now she was in place to notice the coil of rope he'd left behind. But so far she hadn't turned to look in that direction. She reached the second log and walked around it, but in the wrong direction. She went down to go around its base. His trap was near the top, not there at the bottom. She looked at the crows that stood in rows along all the branches. She made a face at them.

One more trap, and if she missed this one, he would have to give chase. If she was rabbit enough, she might be fast. David clenched his teeth as he watched, afraid even to breathe, trying to stay silent. With those long ears, she would hear his slightest motion.

She walked too far left and stepped past the third trap. Then she noticed the rope, curled up on the ground to her right. She looked around but didn't see David. She walked toward the coil of rope he'd left behind. One step right, two steps, three steps, and—*Cuh-rack!*—she stepped into the trap, which was triggered and, in one motion, tightened around her foot and rose high.

Connie was launched into the air upside down.

"Aaahh!" she cried. "Help!"

She tried to pull herself upright to catch at her foot, which was held by the rope to a long tree limb high above.

Crows on the branches beside her cawed.

David stepped into the open.

∾⟡∾

TO Connie, he looked more normal than she had expected. Except he was upside down. Or, rather, she was. The hunter's clothes were almost what Connie would have called a costume from an old movie, but they were well worn and fit him perfectly. On David, they looked like practical hunting clothes. In his hand, he held a bow. To Connie that bow looked giant, as big, almost, as herself. He drew an arrow from a bag on his back and fitted it into the bow.

"Are you going to freeze me?" Connie asked.

"I only hunt animals," he said. "Judging from your ears, I'd say you still have twenty minutes."

"My ears have always been big," Connie responded. The blood was rushing to her head, making her feel strange and dizzy. She was also trying to keep the knapsack up. It pressed against the back of her head.

"Pointy too?" David asked.

Connie put her hands to her ears, surprised. She felt her face next. She had something like a mustache of wiry whiskers over her lips.

"Twenty minutes?" she asked.

He nodded.

"You're a horrible man."

"I'm a cursed man," he corrected her. "You could never understand what that's like. You're much too young."

"No," Connie said. "You're horrible. I see it in your eyes."

"Oh, do you?" David sounded like he was getting upset. "I was nice once too. Do you see that in my eyes? The time I helped a sister and brother like yourself?"

"No," Connie said. "All I see is *mean*."

David raised his shoulders so that his leather vest and his quiver rose.

"It's the curse. As far as you're concerned, I *am* mean. I'm the villain, and I'm the last person you'll ever see."

"You're not a person. You're a monster!" Connie shouted loudly.

"I know it. I was just saying that myself." He frowned.

"And you've got me, but you haven't got Sol!"

"But I will. Sound carries from up here very far." He called, with his hand to his lips, "Did you hear her, Sol? I've got your sister."

"No, you be quiet," Connie said, lowering her voice. She shut her mouth fast.

But it was too late. The hunter stepped into the woods, backward, and almost instantly disappeared from sight.

ACROSS the valley, Connie's first shouts, when she was hoisted up into the air, *had* carried far. Not so far that any deer in the deep woods below would have heard them. They were hardly more than tiny distant cries from some other part of the forest. But there was one deer whose head turned at the sound of those faint cries. It had run long after an elk that it couldn't find, search as it may, and was grazing when it heard the sound—a voice that touched whatever was still human inside of that deer.

The deer immediately ran toward the cries, climbing up rocky parts when it reached the marsh to avoid what it knew now were the marshland's treacherous waters. It climbed by putting its front legs up on a rocky shelf and then pushing off from behind. When it reached level ground, it ran fast the way all deer run, springing off its back legs. It scrambled around a higher pond. It vaulted over dead logs in a series of graceful leaps. It broke through a quarter of a mile of wild hedge, charging through the tangled branches, its antlers ripping through the twiggy mesh without effort.

In the more open parts of the woods, it ran faster than any kid on a bicycle. When it reached the first slope up the mountain, it paused, raised its head, and sniffed. But the breeze was from its back. The wind was carrying the deer's scent forward, to whatever lay ahead, but what lay ahead couldn't be smelled by the deer. There was no way for that deer to see into its future.

As it trotted on, the land rose into stone cliffs many times its height. Trees filled the U-shaped land between the cliffs. It was the obvious way up, along the dry riverbed at the land's center. But this deer chose a different path. With its sharp hooves, it could leap onto tiny rock ledges. It ran along thin stone ramps by the cliffside, where no human could have gone.

CONNIE was grabbing hold of her foot, caught in the rope noose, and held herself up that way. She managed to stay like that for a time, struggling with the well-tied knot, before falling to hang upside down again.

Fur grew on her arms now. Her skin itched.

She was thinking how this had all gone wrong.

She was the one who was supposed to save Sol this time. This had been her time—her chance. And here she was caught again. It was just like he'd said: *Try not to get caught.* She had been upset at him for saying that the other night. She could almost hear Sol's voice now: *I told you so.*

There was a cracking in the brush, and a deer showed itself.

It looked up at her, hanging upside down.

She'd recognize those eyes anywhere, even though they were black and set in a deer's head.

"No, Sol. Run! Get away!" Connie screamed at it. "You're prey now! You can't do anything for me. You've got to save yourself. Please, leave me!"

But her shouts only brought Sol closer. He could sense her fear. But it also sounded as if she didn't want him there anymore. And *that* the deer couldn't believe.

In a fit of panic, Connie bent herself up again to

hold her foot, and she did the only thing she could think of. She clamped her teeth on the rope hard and began to chew.

David, well camouflaged, took aim.

His bow twanged. An arrow flew through the air.

24

THE RIDE

THE THRUSH HAD WAITED for the last moment. It had sat in the trees, jumping from branch to branch, calling out like the other birds. Then, as the hunter put the arrow in and drew the bowstring back, it swooped down, feeling like a hawk diving, although that dive was only a few feet. It struck the bow with all its force as the arrow released. That force wasn't much. The thrush was small compared to the bow.

Connie shut her eyes for a second at the bow's *twang*, then opened them again, terrified of what she would see.

But she didn't see anything except waving branches near where the deer had been and an arrow stuck in a young tree.

She went back to chewing, fast. She found it felt

oddly good. Her teeth were strong, sharp, and long. The rope strands snapped in her mouth. She gnawed as hard as she could, especially sinking her extra-long front teeth in and pushing hard. She felt that acting like a rabbit was making her change faster, but she couldn't worry about that now.

Suddenly her teeth clicked together, top and bottom—she'd chewed totally through the rope—and she fell backward . . . one . . . two seconds, and she struck the ground right on a tree root, which jabbed hard into her lower back below the knapsack. It hurt, but the pain just felt like a wash across her body as she jumped up, and the deer was before her.

It kneeled with its front legs on the ground and its head bowed, its back still standing. Connie understood. She swung a foot over Sol, grabbed the fur of his deer neck with both hands, and lay along his back. He stood at once.

He crashed through branches without pause, his deer head down, even breaking low-hanging limbs off. Connie felt every jarring step as a stab in her back where she'd hit herself in her fall. They were going up through the woods and came out into a stony clearing beyond the last trees. The mountain peak itself rose like a rocky hill just ahead. The land was all rocks now to the top, with a few plants growing from cracks. There was a low point at the top—the pass—and this is where Sol headed. He ran up the open land in a wild zigzag. He jumped up onto a rocky ledge. Connie felt the jolt of his legs as he did and almost slid off. Her arms around his neck, her cheek pressed against him, she clutched him in the tightest hug ever.

"Go, Sol, go," she said into his ear.

The deer turned right and ran quickly along the narrow ledge. Every bounce threatened to throw Connie off his back. To her right, the ledge fell off in a drop now. To her left, a rock wall rose to the highest part of the peak. All the time Connie expected to hear the *twang* of the bow again from below, the *whish* of an arrow, and maybe the *thump* of it striking her or Sol. They were, after all, a clear shot as Sol ran. There were no more trees to hide behind. Once or twice a boulder might have blocked them off from view below.

And David *had* stepped out onto the open rocky land. Sol and Connie were nearing the pass, already a bit far. Some of the crows had taken off into the

air and were circling, cawing, as if cheering at the excitement. They happened to block David's view sometimes too. But he was an expert hunter and besides, if he hit a crow or two, what did it matter? He drew an arrow from his quiver, aimed at the deer running along the stony shelf with the rabbity girl riding on top, and let the arrow fly.

Twang.

Then another. *Twang.*

Then a third, a fourth, and a fifth, shooting very quickly.

THE thrush, when it had struck the hunter's bow, had been hit by the bowstring, which was almost half as thick as the thrush's whole body. The thrush had gone hurtling through the air like an arrow itself. With luck, it managed to start flapping its wings before it hit the ground. It flew in many directions until it finally caught sight of David again uphill, shooting arrows. Then, although it was hurt, it shot forward as fast as it could until it came out past the trees, over rocky land. It aimed for the hunter's weak point. Zooming in, it jabbed him in the neck with its pointy little beak. It felt him flinch in pain. David struck the thrush hard with his palm, knocking it down.

The thrush hit the ground, dazed. But its strike and David's violent swing had done what was necessary—thrown David off his footing. He slipped and fell backward onto the rocks atop his quiver of arrows.

And suddenly the crows leaped off their branches. Crows love to take advantage of *any* animal when it's down—a human hunter too. They swooped over David, a dozen to start, but more flew in fast until the hunter disappeared under a black cloud of wings, beaks, and loud caws. They pecked him mercilessly, even going for his eyes, which he had to cover with his hands. Other crows stayed circling in the air by the peak, cawing loudly at the excitement.

David's bow lay on the ground, forgotten.

But one of the arrows that he had let fly before he'd fallen *hadn't* missed its mark, even though Sol and Connie had been very far off.

David was an excellent shot. His fourth arrow had struck Sol. The arrow had come from so far below that it sliced across the deer's side. It hadn't stuck in, but it cut him deep enough. Sol jumped from the pain, his rear legs slipping off the ledge. For a moment, it looked like they would fall. Connie screamed. Sol the deer leaned forward on his front legs only. His rear legs flailed in the air. He pulled them back up the ledge and kept running, bleeding heavily into his fur.

A hundred yards farther at an uneven limping trot and they reached the mountaintop—the pass. The thrush appeared suddenly, fluttering beside them. Sol ran across the pass, Connie on his back, then down until the accursed valley with the river snaking through it couldn't be seen behind them, only the mountain peak and the sky. The view of the next valley stretched out before them. Sol ran on, stumbling.

Connie worried: Would Sol freeze because he was hit by the arrow? Or did that happen only when it stuck in—did an animal only freeze when it had fallen and was taking its last breaths? And how much time was left before she became a rabbit for real? Five minutes? Less?

"Now we find the place, Sol," Connie said to him. "A brother and sister like us long ago, they left something behind. That *must* be where we're going." She added, "I hope we make it in time."

Connie was shrinking. Her change felt a little like she was falling into a dreamy world that existed right there in a corner of the real one, but that she'd never noticed before. Her hands were shriveling as she watched to tiny, furry feet, but she had to struggle to remember that they weren't supposed to be that way—or that they hadn't been that way sometime in a past she couldn't quite remember. Sol's knapsack was loose on her back. She did her best to hold on to the knapsack by keeping her hands—now her front feet— gripped tightly onto Sol's fur. Her back feet were pushing against the inside of her shoes. She kicked off her shoes and pulled off her socks with her feet. A bit of rope was still tied around her ankle, its end swinging wildly as Sol trotted. She pulled the rope loop off by scratching at it with the other foot. She sank her back feet, complete with claws, into Sol's sides, gripping on gently.

She didn't want to hurt him any more than he was already hurt.

Sol threw his head hard right and left, then climbed down a steep slope carefully. The thrush flew beside him. Rocks came loose and fell far, clattering. Connie was starting to feel like jumping off— dashing down the slope and into the woods ahead. The feeling was strong. It felt like all her troubles would be over. She could run free. It was all she could do to hold on to herself—and Sol.

Sol sprang cautiously off the rocky slope near the

bottom. Connie could feel how his backside hurt by the way he did it. She rode him into the woods and onto a knoll, a small clear hill, the land covered by tiny blue flowers.

"Wait!" Connie shouted.

Connie leaped off Sol's back with a spring and landed, the knapsack bouncing off her into the field. She slid out of her jumper too, which was much too big for her now. The thrush landed nearby.

Connie sniffed the flowers and bit one off, chewing it and swallowing. It tasted good—fresh. But more important, she remembered one of these little blue flowers. From her dream. The manager had been wearing it.

"It must be here," she said. "It must be here somewhere. That was a clue."

Sol had stopped and was licking his wound. Connie worried, watching him. The cut along his side didn't look too bad, not like something Sol would collapse from. But she wasn't sure if he might grow stiff until he froze completely. If that happened, would she ever get him back?

She ran quickly all over, searching for what was left behind. Then she found it, behind a bush—a kind of thicket—growing up against the rock hill that rose to the mountain peak. The entrance to a cave.

"Here! Here!" she called out.

Sol the deer walked over to follow Connie as she hopped into the cave. Light filtered through the entrance but darkness hid the cave's inside. What would turn them back into humans before Sol froze? If he was going to. And before she shrank completely and became a rabbit. Well, she was mostly rabbit already. She felt her head with her front foot. It was furry but still had human-shaped cheeks. Connie hopped all around the dark cave searching.

But all she found was a pile of bones near the back. As her eyes adjusted to the dim light, she could see their outline before her—she was low to the ground now. Some of the bones were curved and some straight. No, not a pile of bones, she thought. A skeleton. She sniffed and felt with her rabbit front paws. The skeleton wasn't human. She could tell that from its shape. She found the skull with a long snout. A deer. Tied around its deer neckbones, which had fallen apart, was a beaded ribbon that she sniffed. It smelled very old. There was only the faintest trace of its own smell left.

The brother long ago had been a deer, thought Connie, like Sol. Connie looked behind her. Sol stood close to the entrance. Was he frozen? No, he still moved. He was licking his wound again.

"The brother didn't make it, Sol," Connie said, although she wasn't sure if he understood her. "The children, they didn't escape. At least not both of them. The boy died, Sol. That's so terrible. The hunter's shot got him after all. *That's* what was left behind."

The sister would have grown up, gotten old, and died too, a very long time ago, Connie thought. She had grown up without her brother.

That was it. The answer to the second riddle.

Connie hopped outside to the knapsack that still lay in the flowers. She dragged it through the cave entrance. She unzipped it using her rabbit teeth and pulled out Sol's cube, also with her teeth and mouth.

Sometimes when she left something with its battery off for a while, it worked again for a short time. She hoped the cube would work now. Connie only needed the answer to the third riddle. She understood the answer to the second one already. *We stick around, the last to go,* and *Used to make needles and fish hooks.* Bones. They'd used bones long ago, she'd heard that before.

"On," she said to the cube. Her voice was starting to squeak.

"Cube on," it said back weakly in Sol's voice, which made Sol the deer look over. "Battery very low. Warning. Plug me in. Battery very low."

"I know. Menu," Connie said carefully. "Puzzle mode. Riddle mode."

"Battery very low. Warning. Shutting down."

"No!" Connie shouted.

The cube paused.

"Shutdown halted. Riddle mode selected. Please state riddle," it said quietly.

"*A world you don't see,*" she said, "*a river you can't hear, more jewels and riches than a king, travel far I'm always near.* Finished."

"Warning. Battery very low. Shutting down. Ten, nine, eight—"

"Stop! Don't shut down. Solve the riddle. Please!"

It paused.

"Shutdown cannot be halted. Seven. Six. Jewels are types of stone. Five. Four. Three. Rivers don't all flow above land. Two. One." The cube spoke once more, very weakly. "Off," it said.

"Are you off?"

There was no answer. The cube's battery was truly dead. She turned to look at Sol the deer.

She understood it all now.

"You're so smart!" she said. "*I'm sometimes called what you are called*. Someone in your family, Sol. A brother. But not you. The boy from long ago. *Used to make fish hooks*. Bones like these, Sol. And the last riddle, a world you don't see full of jewels and with rivers. Underground." Connie stopped to think. "The sister, she had to leave her brother behind. She didn't have time to bury him, Sol. She had to save herself. *We* have to bury him. But—how are we going to without a shovel or something to dig with?"

Connie had tried more than once in her lifetime to dig holes in the ground without a shovel or any tools, just with her bare hands, but it was impossible unless the earth was all mud, which it wasn't here or outside the cave. And certainly she could never dig a hole big enough for all these bones.

Then it struck her. She could do it. Of course she could.

She hopped out of the cave into the light, which seemed bright now, almost blinding, and she looked around the knoll. Where would the sister want her brother buried? With her, of course, normally. But that was hundreds of years ago, and the sister would be buried far away.

What about by the stream that Connie could smell a little ways off through the woods?

She hopped over. Sol followed. There a boulder lay, looking very big to Connie now. At least, it was bigger than she was. That would do. And the ground was softer here too, near the water. She dug quickly. Her claws were sharp and strong as nails. She tossed up a lot of earth between her legs. Soon enough, she moved and dug in a different direction, when the first pile got too high.

As Connie acted more and more like a rabbit, so she became one. She dug for a very long time. Her twenty minutes were up. But she was holding on to her mind, just a little. Or was she? She dug the hole much longer, wider, and deeper than any rabbit hole. But she also began to wander away from it, sniffing and chewing at some wide leaves that grew nearby. She hopped farther from the big hole. When she looked back, a deer was standing over it, its head stretched down. Almost as if it might jump into the hole.

No! Connie thought. Or a rabbit doesn't think a word like *no*, it just thinks the idea *no*. She raced quickly into the cave and began to pull the bones out. She dragged them with her mouth—her long, sharp front teeth over them, her bottom teeth under. She pulled them to the hole and dropped them in. She ran back and forth until she was sure she had taken them all from the back of the cave. Then she pushed the mounds of dug earth into the hole by turning around atop the dirt piles and using her back feet. Once the hole was full, she tapped it down with her legs, over and over again. Sol helped, or anyway he walked over the newly turned black earth, smelling it.

Then the deer and the rabbit looked up, because they heard something coming down the rocky path from the mountain pass.

They saw her, heard her, even smelled her on the breeze with their strong sense of smell as if she really were there that moment: a girl, walking carefully along the ledges, climbing down, hanging on by her hands, choosing her steps. One sleeve was gone from her blouse and her old-fashioned skirt was twisted. Behind her a deer was following, limping, a bloodstained cloth tied against its side, bright red. When they made it off the steep hill, the girl started into the woods, but not the deer. The deer turned aside through the flowers and limped slowly toward the cave.

The girl watched it, then followed. Sol the deer and Connie the rabbit did too. Inside the cave, the deer lay on its side. The sister sat with him. She put her hand on his deer chest, which was rising and falling with short breaths. Until it rose and fell no more. The sister hung her head over the deer, tears from her cheeks falling onto its still form. But her tears couldn't bring her brother back.

She put her face into his fur and held him tight, her arms stretched out far. Then she picked her head up. She stood and dragged the body to the back of the cave. She took a ribbon that held her skirt tied in back—it was small, beaded, and red—and fastened it around the deer's neck. She spoke to the cave, almost as if she knew someone else was there.

"I've no time or strength to carry my brother to a proper place, cave. I'm so sorry. Take care of him! I must go on." She was crying. "Please, someone lay him to rest one day. If you do this, I grant you whatever it is you will, or need, in this dreadful place."

She walked out of the cave, right by the rabbit and

deer that watched her and followed her. She walked over the little blue flowers, crushing them flat under her feet—as if she really were there. Until she reached the boulder and stream beside the mound of freshly turned earth. She stepped into that stream and walked with her feet in the water because she knew that is what to do when you are chased. Walking in water leaves no footprints or smells.

No one could follow her or know where she went.

Shortly after, something else happened. And this was something that had never happened before.

The deer came out of the cave looking like a wild animal, no ribbon on its neck.

It walked across the knoll. Its steps didn't crush the blue flowers it walked on. It seemed almost to be held up by their fragile stems. It walked right to the boulder and stepped into the stream, just like its sister had. She may have left no trace, but her little brother knew where she'd gone. The deer walked, the water covering its ankles, until it disappeared downstream behind the trees.

<hr>

SOL and Connie were granted what they needed most. The change back was quick, although for Connie it was painful. Shrinking never hurt, it seemed, but growing did. So Sol grew smaller and back to a boy quietly and easily, the gash on his chest healing as he did, while Connie writhed, twisted, and called out in pain as she grew from a rabbit to a girl again. Until finally she gave a sigh of relief, lying on her side.

Sol walked to the cave and came out with his pants and a shirt on again, barefoot, carrying his knapsack. He found that he remembered everything from being a deer, what he'd heard, what he'd seen, most important, what he'd felt.

By that time, Connie had gotten her jumper from where it lay over the tiny blue flowers, and she'd pulled it over her head.

They walked, hand in hand, to the grave. The freshly turned black earth had deer and rabbit footprints all over it, crisscrossing. That was odd to see.

Beside the grave lay an old blackened ribbon.

"Oh no," Connie said, "I forgot to bury it with him."

"It's okay," said Sol. "Maybe we should keep it. Who knows? Maybe we're supposed to."

He picked it up and stuck it into the knapsack.

A tweet sounded from overhead. A little wood

thrush, brown with black spots on its white chest, was darting over from the field of tiny blue flowers.

～❦～

THEY followed the bird downhill through the woods and to a wide brook. The thrush stopped there to drink, but neither Sol nor Connie would dare it. Crossing the brook in bare feet, they marched on, following an obviously beaten path. It was the first sign of civilization. Others had trod here. The sun shone overhead—it was a warm day.

A long time later, they came out to a narrow road winding down from the mountain. The first vehicle to pass was a pickup truck. Sol and Connie flagged it down like two children hoping to be rescued. The truck slowed and pulled over to the side. The passenger door opened and out stepped a young man with just the wisp of a beard. The driver came out too, another young man, with blond hair and no whiskers growing on his face at all.

"Is everything okay?" the wispy-bearded one asked.

The blond glanced around at the woods.

"Where are you coming from?" he asked. "Is there a trail here? Where are your parents?"

Sol spoke, his voice scratchy and wavering, but human.

"We're lost," he said. "We could use a hand."

"What, have you been camping in the woods?"

"You look pretty rough," the blond said.

"Are you hurt?" asked the bearded one.

"No," Sol said. "At least not too bad. We're just scratched up."

The truth is that Sol and Connie looked like they'd been struggling through the woods for days or weeks. They were scratched almost everywhere. Their clothes were dirty and torn. Their hair stuck out in all directions. They were both barefoot. They looked very much like what they were, lost children.

The blond reached into his pocket and pulled out a phone. He checked it. "We've got a signal."

He handed it to Sol.

"You call whoever you need to call."

"I don't know the number," Sol said. "Wait, I know the name of the city."

He called the number for information, got past the computer to reach a human operator, and told the operator their aunt's name and the city she lived in. The number was listed. The operator told it to him. Sol didn't need to write it down. Nor did he ask her for an automatic connection. He wanted to prove something to himself. He repeated it back to her once, knew he had it memorized already, hung up, and dialed.

"Hello?" A woman's voice answered.

"Hello? Aunt Heather? It's Sol."

"Sol?" The voice sounded surprised. "My nephew Sol?"

"Yes, your nephew. Solomon."

There was a pause. "Long time. How are you? Where are you calling from?"

"Well, um, we're coming to visit you."

"We?" There was a pause. "Connie? And your father?"

"Just me and Connie."

The bearded man was pulling on Sol's arm. He took Sol behind the truck and pointed to the license plate.

Sol nodded.

"We're getting a ride," Sol said. "Do you have a pen and paper? Let me give you the license plate of the guys who are bringing us."

Sol read it out. Then the man handed Sol his

driver's license too, and, gesturing at the blond, got his driver's license and handed it to Sol. Sol read off their names, addresses, and all the information from the licenses he could find.

The bearded man took the phone from him.

"You're the kids' aunt?" Sol and Connie heard him asking.

There was a conversation about where they were, and the young man seemed to be making sure the kids were expected. Apparently Aunt Heather said yes.

When they hung up, the blond gave the phone to Sol.

"You hang on to it, okay? Anyone you want to call, go ahead and do it."

And so Sol and Connie got into the pickup, the narrow seats in the back. But before they did, the thrush jumped up onto the side of the truck and sang loudly.

Connie said to it, "You'll tell her everything, won't you? We've got to keep going."

The thrush tweeted confidently, launched into the air, and darted away.

Sol and Connie watched it go.

So did the men.

Soon they were talking as they drove along the curving road.

"We weren't doing anything else today," said the blond one, who was the driver. His name was Marc. "Were we, Harris?" he asked the other one.

"Nah," said Harris, the bearded one. "In fact, I think we were headed this way. West."

"Yes, well, we were headed *in* that direction."

The two laughed.

They drove through countryside, then towns, then more countryside, then more towns. They got to talking, and Sol and Connie ended up telling them the whole story, starting at the beginning, with Holaderry in Grand Creek, through coming out onto the road today.

"Nah!" and "What did you do then?" were just a few of the things that the two men said as Sol and Connie told the story.

Sol took out Holaderry's journal too, which they still had, and read from the dried-out, wavy pages.

"You've got Marc's stories beat, a hundred percent," said Harris, stroking his beard.

"And the journal," Marc said. "It's really impressive that you've got that thing. Leather-bound and all."

"With the loopy handwriting," Harris said. "As if it were really written by the *evil Holaderry*."

"You mean you don't believe us?" Sol asked.

"Now, we didn't say that, did we? One thing, though," Marc said. "If I were you, I wouldn't tell that story to, you know, everyone. Or show that journal around."

"I agree," Harris said, giving several quick nods.

25

AUNT HEATHER

AUNT HEATHER LIVED in a small gray house. She looked at them curiously when she opened the door. She had intelligent eyes, but that wasn't surprising. Her sister—Sol and Connie's mother—had been a scientific genius.

But Sol remembered less his aunt's intelligence than her black hair cropped at the chin, her angling cheeks, and her thick, dark brows. He had been so young the last time he'd met her, it was only natural that he mainly remembered how she looked.

"Come in," she said.

She invited Marc and Harris in too, but they politely said they had to go. She tried to give them money. "For the gas," she added. But they refused absolutely, mumbling something about doing "their part."

Once they were gone, Aunt Heather sat Sol and Connie down on a couch covered with pillows of many different colors.

She said, "I couldn't reach your father anywhere. His number's disconnected, and all his online and email accounts are closed." She patted Sol on the shoulder. She didn't want to say that she'd always known Sol and Connie would face trouble in their life. She said instead, "You two are welcome here as long as need be. Life is full of surprises," she said, more to herself than to them. "You two might know that already." She pulled back her lips. "You really look terrible."

"We feel terrible," Connie said.

"Well, when you called, I started thinking about going out to eat. Chinese or something. You see, I'm a vegetarian. There's not much in the fridge for you two, I'm afraid. Just veggies and beans. But seeing how you look, maybe we have to clean you up first. And bandage some of your cuts too."

"We can do a lot of it," Sol said. "We know how to take care of ourselves."

"And we're okay with veggie-tarian," Connie said.

"Neither of us feel like meat today, Aunt Heather," Sol agreed.

"Really? You're just being polite."

"No," Sol said. "No meat. Maybe tomorrow."

Aunt Heather nodded.

"I can see you'll have to tell me all about your adventure." She looked at them. "Tomorrow."

THE thrush fluttered up the street. It reached the shop with the sign above that said ALL CREATURES, BIG AND SMALL.

CLOSED said a smaller sign in the window.

The thrush tap-tap-tapped on the windowpane.

After a short time, the door opened. Gertrude stood there, big as a bear, leaning on her cane.

The thrush flew in over her head.

"You made it!"

She thumped her cane and looked at the thrush. She grinned.

The thrush sang back.

"I knew it." She corrected herself. "I didn't know it, but I suspected it. Tell me."

Gertrude shut the door and took her seat by the till. Her fingers curled around the duck's-head handle of her cane. Her face grew serious as the thrush tweeted and sang. Gertrude's knee even went up and down nervously.

"Well, my riddles helped them, didn't they?" she said. And later, "Yes, I was afraid that they'd believe Monique. She can be so convincing." And later again, "David's a mean fellow. Always was. Sounds like you gave him what he had coming, and the crows too. I'm glad the crows were with us, this time." She closed her eyes, then opened them. "And Sol and Connie? They got off okay?"

She listened to the bird's singing.

"I'm so glad. They're survivors, aren't they?" She

made a sound in her throat almost like a laugh, though it wasn't. "Okay, I know you're tired. And I know the important parts now. You go. You rest."

She walked to the front shop window and turned the sign on it over, so it said OPEN again to those who passed by.

"I think it's time to get back to regular business," she said. Then added to herself, in a very low voice, "The struggle goes on."

She stepped to the door and opened it.

The thrush flew outside. It darted at once into the tree by the shop where many other birds were calling. The time was late afternoon already, almost sunset, a time for birdsong. The thrush was very tired. It had been awake for two days straight. It had never done that before. It seemed to the thrush like it had been awake for months. Years!

But it wasn't ready to sleep yet, not after all the excitement. It called to the other birds, many of them also thrushes. It wanted to tell them its story: its struggles against the stormy wind and over the mountain, its visit to the terrible witch's cabin, the hawk circling in the air. It would tell about its mistakes too, losing Connie in the river, and the hard decision it had had to make. But how, in the end, it had fought the hunter and led the children to safety.

Just as it had been asked to. No matter how small it was and how much it had doubted that it would ever succeed. There had been many times when it had almost given up hope. It would be sure to mention those times too.

And then, just before falling asleep—and not telling any of its story after all, it was so tired—the thrush thought, I *was* the hero of the story, after all.

CHAPTER

IT SHOULD HAVE
BEEN OBVIOUS

IN THE CENTRAL ROOM of the lodge, Monique and
David sat, listening to a chorus of frogs outside and
watching the fire Monique had lit in the hearth.
Around them stood animals of all kinds—once kids—
frozen and posed in odd positions. The flickering fire
was the only light in the lodge besides a candle David
had set on a side table. The candle's glow, as he put it
down, lit the welts, bites, scratches, and scabs all over
his arms and face, and the little patches of white on
his skin too. He'd already rubbed some cream that
Monique had made for him into his wounds.

Monique had combed out her long hair—no more
ponytail. It fell over the back of the cushioned chair
on which she sat. Her green cap hung on a hook in
shadows by the door.

David sat in the big chair directly in front of the fire, his hand on the unmoving fox beside the chair. He scratched the fox absentmindedly.

"Not only did you let those two get away," Monique said to him, "but you know they've got the witch Fay Holaderry's journal with them?"

"Do they?" David asked. "I never saw it. Besides, what does it matter? No one believes those things."

Monique pulled the corners of her lips back. It was a look of impatience and dissatisfaction. David knew that look well.

"You wouldn't be keeping some journal yourself, would you?" she asked. "Some diary, secret from me?"

David kept staring at the fire.

"Why would I do that?" he asked finally.

"Telling kids it's all my fault, that I'm to blame, that you just got roped into this? Now, *that* no one would ever believe. Just remember, all I ever did was turn the kids to animals."

David leaned back, looked at her, and even smiled, though not in a happy way—more as a peace offering.

"I know it, and I admit it. My fate's my own fault and no one else's."

They stared into each other's eyes until finally turning to watch the fire again.

Monique got up and put another log on. She picked up a poker and stoked the fire, crouching down and blowing it to life.

"I tried my best, you know," David said. "You know I did. I came this close to getting them both." He shook his head. There was a long silence. Only the fire spoke.

Monique still looked upset.

"What would you think," David said at last, "if we moved Nicki"—he pointed to one of the wolves—"back near the window, where she was long ago, remember? And we could take Alexandra here"—he pointed to a white and tawny-brown weasel—"and give her a spot where she catches the morning light. And Jacob the bear could stand more naturally, on four feet, and we could take Herman here and put him on top, and spread his wings."

Monique smiled a little.

"Actually," she said, "I was thinking of Herman near the bedroom doorway, and Alexandra facing him, on her back legs. But Jacob would look good on all fours again, I agree, like a proper bear." She sighed through her nose. "We really could use some new ones, though." She pulled her hair back as if making a ponytail, then let it drop. "Try harder next time."

The two of them spent the evening rearranging the animals of the lodge, trying out new poses and new places, and putting logs on the fire from time to time. David brushed many of the animals, since they were getting dusty. He was careful never to look at his quiver of arrows hanging near the hearth, where, at the bottom, lay all his secrets.

⁓∽⊱∘⊰∾⁓

SOLOMON and Constance Blink washed, cleaned up, and were shown to what their aunt Heather called the "guest room."

"There's only one mattress," Aunt Heather said.

"We don't mind sharing," Sol answered.

She looked surprised, but all she said was, "Good. Good night, you two." Then, pausing, she stepped into the room and gave them each a kiss on the forehead.

"Good night," Connie and Sol both said.

Once they were alone, Connie asked, "How much do we tell her?"

"I don't know, Connie. Maybe everything?"

"Or maybe we just make up a story," Connie said.

Before they lay down, Sol unpacked the things they had left with them. Holaderry's journal, *How to Cook and Eat Children*, which, strange to say, had saved them in the cabin. Their mother's last scientific paper. His Know-It-All Cube. Connie had told him everything about how much it had helped her, how it had spoken to her with his voice—and how that had made her feel better. They still had the paperback book, *The Mismeasure of Man*, that for some reason Connie had repacked although it was chewed to pieces. The pocketknife, rusted shut, that Theo would never need again. The old, darkened ribbon. A pencil. The empty water bottle that would go straight to recycling. And the Valentine's Day card Sol had gotten last year at school from a secret admirer.

He stared at that last item, long and hard, opened it, and read it: *Dear Sol, Will you be my valentine? Love, Your Secret Valentine.* Sol was supposed to be so brilliant, but he hadn't seen it this whole time—the obvious, staring him in the face.

He gave Connie a look.

"I was going to tell you," she said. "I just never found the right time." She hesitated. "Are you mad?"

"No, Connie, of course not." Sol shook his head. "It's perfectly logical. Of all the kids in our old school,

292

who was most likely to have left me a card like that, hidden in my desk?" He stared at the card. "I should have recognized those hearts too, right away." He closed the card. "Thank you, Connie," he said.

Connie tried to be polite. "You're welcome." She had a huge smile on her face.

So they turned off the light and lay down to sleep together in the same bed. But light still shone through the window. It wasn't very dark in the bedroom here in the city.

"We won't be fooled next time," Connie said, still awake.

"No," Sol told her. "Definitely not."

ACKNOWLEDGMENTS

Acknowledgments are due Angelika for being there from the beginning to the end, for all her help, tremendous support, patience, and love.

Many good friends gave me incredible advice and help: Stacie Heintze; Ruth, Ben, Louis, Walter, and Sara Teitelbaum; Heather Nelson; Shaun Cutts; Jeffrey Feola. Thanks to more readers and helpers in many ways: Padhrig McCarthy; Karl, Marlo, Jonah, and Rebecca Isaac; Johanna Striar; William, Nancy, Benjamin, and Rachel Weiss. Thanks also to Anastasia Portnoy, Dave Merzin, and Harry Merzin; Elizabeth Klein; Cindy Axinn Newberg; Steven Hecht; and Corey Black. Of course, Jeff McGowan; Kim Sobel; Ben and Simcha McGowan; Seth, Kathy, Ethan, and Jacob McGowan; Judee Rosenbaum; Stefanie Nohalka and Michael Kandler; Silvia, Peter,

Jasmin, and Alina Schiefer; and Ilse and Stefan Nohalka. Thank you, Barbara Dax, for your support. So many thanks obviously to CO and ENIV.

Vielen herzlichen Dank Mika und Wolfgang Kauders, Monika Beckmann, Beate Wegerer, Barbara Eichinger, Martina Adelsberger und den Bibliotekarinnen und Bibliothekaren der Büchereien Wien, die mich so unterstützen.

A very special thank-you is due Thurber House in Columbus, Ohio—where part of this book was written in James Thurber's well-furnished attic—for their incredibly generous residency and support. Words are not enough. Thanks to Pat Shannon, Meg Brown, Tricia Fairman, Anne Touvell, and Susanne Jaffe.

I am very grateful to Kelly Joyce, who read every draft of this book, gave counsel, guidance, and wisdom, and without whom I could never have written this book.